# UNTOLD LIES

## A PERSONAL JOURNEY TO THE TRUTH

> As someone who has made choices that often challenged convention, I enjoyed Raga's story. Many will see reflections of their own lives and feel encouraged. Untold Lies is a book everyone should read!
>
> *- Milind Soman*

STORYOEMS—WHEN STORIES BECOME POEMS

# UNTOLD LIES

## A PERSONAL JOURNEY TO THE TRUTH

### RAGA OLGA D'SILVA

*My dearest Seema,*

*You are MY MAGIC!*

*Thank you for your love!*

*Raga* ఆ౦ళ

## EMBASSY BOOKS
www.embassybooks.in

Untold Lies © Raga Olga D'silva

First Edition 2019

Published in India by:
Embassy Book Distributors
120, Great Western Building,
Maharashtra Chamber of Commerce Lane,
Fort, Mumbai 400 023, India
Tel: (+9122) -30967415, 22819546
Email: info@embassybooks.in
www.embassybooks.in

ISBN: 9789388247641

Cover Design by Sonal Churi

Layout and typesetting by Sonal Churi & Brand Soul Creations

Illustration by Sunil Pujari

Photo credits:
Artisan Jewellry : Anil Bharwani
Photography : Pooja Moolchandani
Make up: Samruddhi Sathe
Co-ordination: Rashi Prakriti

Printed & Bound in India by Quarterfold Printabilities., Navi Mumbai

# TESTIMONIALS

---

66 Raga like the musical notes unravels her magic. She is truly the light in the room; she embraces you without boundaries and connects from the soul.

I've had the opportunity to meet and interact with Raga professionally through the years, and yet I couldn't read her void. The untold lies that were brewing in her mind, where she was a prisoner for many years.

When I read the book, I could breathe slow and fast, connect with the characters in more ways than one. The beauty of Untold Lies is the fact that we as humans at many levels are hiding truths from ourselves at the very basic level. We are absorbing from the society and becoming social animals, without listening to our own instinct.

Raga braves her demons and demonstrates strength and triumph in the chapters you will read. She celebrates love without compartments, and divisions and rules. She cheerleads positivity and the proverbial light at the end of the tunnel. Seeing the journey of Raga, I can only imagine what she has gone through to sum up the courage, and to talk about love the way she does.

Read and you'll find out the traps in which lie your own personal "Untold Lies". 99

*- Kubra Sait*

---

" The best thing in life is "love" and yet there is "fear" always attached to it. That is the irony of life. And love. In these beautiful poems and stories or should I say "storyoems", Raga Olga D'Silva brings out the beauty of these two emotions in a poignant and evocative manner, in words simply told. Perhaps a first of its kind, this collection is heart-warming. "

*- Nandita C Puri*
Author (Nine On Nine, Two Worlds and Unlikely hero: Om Puri)

---

" These stories were like balm to my soul.

We accrue so many wounds through life's journey. And then we cover them and hide them – we believe they are our shame, so that instead of healing they multiply and grow till in the end we ourselves become one giant scar tissue.

Untold Lies has been the healing light breaking through those self-imposed shrouds of shame and guilt, the magic touch that soothes and comforts and dries my tears so I can be whole again... "

*- Seema Anand*
Mythologist | Master Storyteller | Expert on the KamaSutra

---

" Raga Olga D'silva's book is titled Untold Lies but it might well be called Told Truths. Her storyoems are truthful to the core. A voice that deserves to be heard...whether in prose or poetry. "

*- Wendell Rodricks*

" Raga is a woman who sees the world through the eyes of a girl with wonder and with curiosity. Raga's collection of stories and poems is realistic, poignant and it is not just girls or women who can relate to it. Raga's experiences are universal in some ways and her emotions expressed are emotions that are traditionally suppressed and to express them candidly takes courage and an authenticity of soul that is so evident in Raga's narrative. Raga's experiences as penned down will encourage girls and young women to be free from these experiences and build a life that they will be proud of. This collection of stories and poems 'Untold Lies' is authentic, cathartic, experiential and could make young women braver in every aspect.

Reading Raga's book, I remembered this "Poetry is the journal of the sea animal living on land, wanting to fly in the air. Poetry is a search for syllables to shoot at the barriers of the unknown and the unknowable. Poetry is a phantom script telling how rainbows are made and why they go away." — Carl Sandburg, from The Atlantic, March 1923. "

*- Dr Annurag Batra*

Author, writer, TV show host, Angel investor and entrepreneur, and most Importantly MBA (Much Below Average)

# TABLE OF CONTENTS

# PREFACE

———————————

We all have a little girl in us. Our lives are shaped by incidents that are experienced during that little-girl phase and we live that story all our lives.

We get labelled and we carry those labels throughout our lives until the little girl in us realises that life is beyond all that labelling. The process of discovery and change starts to happen later, when we allow ourselves to unlearn and re-learn and then create new experiences. These labels are expressed on a day-to-day basis through our behaviour, actions and reactions and how we are as people.

The idea of writing a book of poems never occurred to me. There is a huge part of me that lives in fear of being judged because of the choices I made. These choices have come from a place of love; yet there is that big F word – FEAR. This duality of living my truth yet living a lie has had a huge impact on me as a person. Some of my relationships have been impacted by this one untold lie which I learnt to express through poems and my storytelling.

It was only after my friends and family started encouraging me to share the message that I had the courage to speak. My twins and partner in particular felt it was important for me to use my experiences to demonstrate that love is all that matters.

I realised that there were labels that were being inherited by me and none of them were truly me. Those who thought they knew me handed them over to me and I believed them to be true. With time I realised that they really weren't mine any more.

These labels kept me restrained from putting forth my narrative for a long time. Poetry helped me express them; every poem had a story in it.

This is when it felt right to author a book that was different - with stories in the background that eventually became poems and that's how I came up with the idea of 'storyoems' – stories that become poems.

This book is a collection of stories and poems that were the key to creating a complete person. Some broken, some healed, some in the process of healing.

The 'Untold Lies' expresses that little girl's journey of labels and the key incidents that shaped her life.

The individual poems may not perfectly relate to the various short stories I have shared but these are poems that live inside of us, from the lessons we have learnt from these experiences, the stories that we carry inside. We are all stories and poems in our own way.

The little girl goes through her journey in this book through nine stories. The first story focuses on the event that had the biggest impact on her life, when the lies were discovered as a young woman. That night was the turning point perhaps; when the easy way of living; of sitting on the fence was questioned. Emotions were on a high that night; perhaps a culmination of things that is inside us, the knowing that things are on the cusp of change. The young woman allowed those emotions to let go through her as she pondered over life's choices.

She becomes that little girl again as she goes into her past and seeks the answers. Slowly through the short stories she discovers the key labels that marked their presence and that process helped her to un-learn.

The little girl has a secret she is hiding and takes the readers on a journey of living her truth, through her stories of hunger, hurt, fear, pain, punishment, loneliness, love and finally finds the strength to understand her truth before she accepts and then lives it.

The poems express the various emotions that one goes through in life. There are many observational poems on everyday life. There are poems on heartbreak, the pain of the broken pieces and the hurt that lingers on. However, each poem is full of hope and that is what I would like to leave with the readers.

It is obvious that the little girl, now a grown woman, wakes up every now and again in the middle of the night and reflects on life – sometimes, amused by it, at times simply accepting, through her 3 am poems.

Her mother who stood for everything magical in her life plays a significant role in shaping her life's story.

It is in the final story that the truth is revealed and the untold lies are unfolded.

It has taken fifteen years for the little girl in me to speak the truth and I am grateful that I could do so in this lifetime.

Thank you to those who love me unconditionally and those who don't. Both offer me something each day to look forward.

There will be no more untold lies.

# UNTOLD LIES

"Arrrhhhhhhhhhhhhh," her screams reverberated through the large, three-bedroom house in the suburbs of Wellington in beautiful New Zealand - a country that was now her home. In the dark night, half asleep, with half-opened eyes, terror-stricken, she could see the silhouette of someone holding a shiny blade in her hands. The smell was familiar, she knew this person for sure, her entire being went rigid as she recognized the person standing so close to her. She could smell the anger, she sensed the depth of frustration and deep anguish - emotions that drove someone to make dramatic choices without thought, even if it meant holding a knife to someone they loved.

"Mummmmmmmy, what are you doing?" she managed to whisper, as she heard the young twins stir due to the commotion around them. Keeping an eye on the woman standing in front of her, ready to plunge the knife; she softly patted the twins to sleep. "Shh babies, it's all good. Mama is here with you. Love you." Comforted, they fell back asleep.

It was ironic that in that room, in the darkness, it was all about mothers and their children. It was about love.

Yet, one mother had a shiny sharp blade in her hand, ready to end it all for all those present in that bedroom. Both mothers were protecting the ones they loved.

"What's going on mummy?" she asked again. "If you put that knife down, perhaps we can have a talk?"

She could see the shiny blade menacingly making its way down to the side of her mother. Very slowly. In the dark, it all looked so dramatic. The sound of the distant silence and her pulsating heartbeat, combined with the heartbeats of three others in the room, made a powerful presence. It felt like darkness had a voice suddenly.

Afraid, awkward, shocked and fearful, she went out to the living room as she was too uncomfortable to put the lights on. She didn't want to see her mother like this, nor did she want her mother to see her this way. Somewhere deep inside, she knew why her mother was so upset. She wanted to put it out there, yet she didn't. Darkness was her best friend at this point. Even if it meant that she ended up with the sharp, shiny thing inside her heart, she wasn't prepared to show her face to her mother.

"I have no words to express my deepest embarrassment at your actions," the mother said. "You are worse than a slut. At least a slut has morals. You have no morals. You are a married woman with children, yet you are doing this." As the mother threw some papers at her, she felt her anger.

"Please keep your voice down!" she cried. "The babies will wake up and so will the neighbours."

But worrying about others wasn't at the top of her mother's mind that night. She was like a caged lion. "You! You are a disgrace to me, to this family, to the world! You selfish b###h! Where is the gratitude? What happened to loyalty? What happened to my dutiful little girl? "

She would have preferred the knife at that point. These words knifed through her and pierced her soul. She knew what it was about and yet there wasn't much she could say or do. She was at the mercy of her loved one that night. Her soft dark hair, styled to suit her oval face was a mess that night. Her usual soft eyes, were full of fear, pain and a strange sense of the guilt seeping through, making them even darker brown than usual. Her lips had a strained look. As she stood up, her tiny frame of five feet and an inch, looked even smaller.

Slowly, with her head bowed, she whispered, "Do what you need to do." She felt a loud thud on her face. The slap was loud enough to wake the neighbours, she thought. Unafraid, she simply sat, waiting for the next blow, as she realised there was nothing left to say.

In the noise of the otherwise silent night, another figure appeared. It was the husband. "What's going on?" he asked.

In his voice, one could hear the emptiness of the night and the silent acceptance of things that are on the cusp of change; a knowing that things would never be the same again. She knew this. He knew this.

Your soul knows before you accept. Life is an interesting journey and it's all backwards. They say it's all written and then we live our lives. The soul already knows the things that are meant to happen - the feelings, the emotions, the actions and the reactions. We think we live forward each day, but each day, we live finitely backwards, playing the story in reverse.

That's how it felt, watching the husband and the mother standing there. Both had many emotions on their faces that dark night, but they had one emotion in common; they both looked disappointed.

She could hear her mentor's words from the past. "Now, amongst all the emotions that we believe someone reacts to, the one emotion that affects us all deeply is when we feel that others are disappointed in us. Disappointing others is like falling in someone's eyes; it's seen as failing and failing is considered so negative in our lives. Live a good life. Work hard at trying not to disappoint others or yourself."

That night, in that silence and in that noise, she felt herself failing, she had disappointed those who loved her and those she cared about deeply, she had strived so hard to be a good wife, a good daughter and a good mother. She had succeeded in so many ways, and yet in being true to them, she had failed to be fully true to herself. She had lived so many untold lies.

The voice in her head boomed again, "In life, there are certain times you cannot go back. Once this time passes, you can never get it back. It's gone. It's over. There will be other times. But this time won't stay. It's moved on before you know it. Like when you drink too much alcohol. Once you are drunk, you can't go back to not being drunk until it passes." This was that moment, she realised. She could not undo what had happened. It had been done. There was nothing that could reverse it - not the action or the reaction. This was the reality she had to live with and those in the room that night had to do so as well.

We don't understand the consequences our choices have on our lives and on those of people around us until we live through them completely. Each choice we make is like a step taking us to the next part of our life. Some steps have a significant impact in our lives but all steps take us somewhere forward, even if we don't realise it at that moment. These steps are like time, which keeps going; it keeps moving ahead.

The husband, showing only remorse and no aggression, came towards her, she won't ever forget that voice. He quietly said, "Are these your words, have you written this?"

She stared at the words in front of her: words she had written to someone. She remembered every sentence, these words had taken her away from the reality of her life, from being a mother, a wife and a daughter in a foreign land in a job that made her a star but was monotonous. The words took her to a world that she could fabricate, a world she could create, just like one did when one closed one's eyes, just as she used to when she was a kid, laying next to her dad. Except, in this case, it was with her eyes wide open - a dream that was slowly turning into a nightmare for all.

She had known for a long time that her marriage was over; both knew but pretended not to. The emptiness in her was there, every day, she had tried very hard to make it work - but there was still a very deep void. Perhaps she had not found the love within; perhaps her expectations were not right, but she felt the emptiness inside. Outwardly she was full of life and shared her joy with the world, but on the inside, she felt herself withering away on a day-by-day basis.

"Yes," she responded quietly. What happened next will remain a blur, voices, noises, in that room that night; it smelt of smoke, although no one was smoking. It was smoke from burnt anger, hurt, pain, disappointment, shock, jealousy and hatred. The after effect was the same: everything had turned to ash.

Night turned to day, there wasn't much said, only felt. Everyone was resigned to the story of last night. Morning came as usual, the night had defined the rest of her life ahead. Twins off to school, mother in the kitchen, husband off to work, she, off to her day ahead. Nothing had changed and yet everything had.

She lived in her head, that was the space that occupied her more than she occupied it. She had lived her life as if it was a film that she was a part of. She thought of herself in the third person. Nothing in it was happening to her; it was all part of someone's plot and she was just a mere actor in it. At times, she was a director and at times, simply a technician changing the lights.

Last night had been different. She couldn't be in that movie as a third person. This was her movie, her life, her choices, her pain, her guilt and her reality. And she had to make choices, unconventional choices, choices that would shake the fabric of most families.

That night was the beginning of many such days and nights. With this new acceptance, she would be giving the world permission to judge her. The choice wasn't easy. She knew that the pain that her choices would cause wasn't going to be easy. Would she be strong enough to see her loved ones in pain from these choices? Her fear wasn't about what she had to endure from this world; her fear was about what her family would go through because of her choices. Would she find the strength inside to stay authentic to herself and, in doing so, to her family? Would the guilt kill her before she moved ahead? Would people still love her for who she was? Where would it take her and her children? So many questions crept into her head that morning.

The tension continued for long days and even longer nights. She tried to hold on to the family, but the darkness had already taken its toll. Or perhaps it was showing the way towards the light for all. Truth is light, but the path is not always lit, that was the path she had chosen to follow.

She had no idea when it all started. She had always lived a full life, being the kind of person whose energy walks in before they do and stays much after they have left. She felt attracted to all kinds of people all her life. People fascinated her and many found her childlike, yet mature outlook fascinating. She was rebellious, yet she followed order. She was disciplined and yet disorderly at times. She could easily laugh, but it was hard for her to cry. She loved fully and yet could be aloof. So it wasn't much of a surprise that when she loved she just loved. Or so she thought. She simply felt attracted to energies and then she followed through. Perhaps that was the biggest lie she told herself.

**Or were there other, untold lies?**

**She thought, perhaps it was time to reveal the story that started the lies.**

# UNTOLD LIES

You see my smiling face
With laughter lines and crinkly eyes.

In this unemotional race,
Do you ever see the untold lies?

My steps feel weak and strong,
My heart tries to right the wrong.

In this world full of lies and dark skies,
Do you ever see the Untold lies?

You see my smiling face,
With laughter lines and crinkly eyes.

In this unemotional race,
Do you ever see the untold lies?

My thoughts sprinkle their pieces on the floor,
My pieces scatter and slide through the closed door.

In the duality of our truth that stays as lies,
Do you ever see the unseen drops in my eyes?

You see my smiling face,
With laughter lines and crinkly eyes.

In this unemotional race,
Do you ever see the untold lies?

My eyes talk more than they see,
My heart feels more than it beats.

In the blanket of the dark deep skies,
We end up living your untold lies.

# ON THE PODIUM OF LIFE

The bell rings loudly and silently,
With all its sadness and its glee.

On this podium of life, what do I see?
I ask, "How many breaths are truly left in me?"

My eyes search for those who withstood the storm,
I search and find them all standing forlorn.

My broken pieces, they have embraced,
Of pain, of suffering, my life has graced.

They look up to me with gratitude,
As through my brokenness, they found their fortitude.

My eyes thank them as they look up my way.
In that moment I walk on with nothing left to say.

My eyes search for those who broke me,
All will some day become a part of my history.

There he was, all morose and sad,
Asking for forgiveness for the times we had.

There she was, standing sullenly,
Did she know she had hurt me knowingly?

My broken pieces had spread far and wide,
Some I still talk about, most I hide.

I move on from them and more as I continue to slide,
How many more breaths left on this podium of life?

My eyes search for the ones whom I caused pain,
They were standing there staring in vain.

Those whose hearts I broke with a smile,
Those whose struggles I understood but only for a while.

Then there were those who were hurt by my hurt but still kept on,
Those were the most painful because hurt lingers on.

I force myself to walk ahead, not look back with strife,
As I reflect on how many breaths I have left on the
podium of life.

# EMPTY BOTTLES MAY I ASK?

Looking at you, I can't help but think,
How much emptiness have you filled?

In those moments of madness, ending in a blink,
How much emptiness have you really filled?

When you get consumed and they hit the floor,
Does it make you stop them and show them the door?

Looking at you, I can't help but think,
How much emptiness have you filled.

When the noise levels increase and the silence loses its sound,
Do you stop them and turn them around?

Looking at you, I can't help but think,
How much emptiness have you filled?

When they empty you until their emptiness gets filled,
Do you stop them before they get themselves killed?

Looking at you, I can't help but think,
How much emptiness have you filled?

Look at you. In your own emptiness, you kill,
Look at them. Those who empty you remain empty still.

# BE LIKE THE SUN

May laughter reach those eyes,
And hide those painful lies.

That soul-wrenching pain you feel,
Let not your shine it steal.

Keep walking with head held high,
Look up as your eyes search the sky.

There is your answer, you know,
Be like the sun; put on a show.

May happiness feed your soul,
And hide that deep, ghastly hole.

That despairing cry that whispers through,
Let it out; don't let it brew.

Walk like there is no tomorrow,
Be like the sun; put on a show.

Shine like you carry a billion lights,
Give up this pain; give up this fight.

Spread warmth and happiness wherever you go,
Put your best suit on with a tie or a bow.

Smile with the truth only you know,
Be like the sun; put on a show.

# THE BOXES OF LIFE

Year-ends and experiences assorted,
The boxes come out to be re-sorted.

The box of challenges is the first to be cleaned;
It has learning and wisdom with folded hands to be gleaned.

This box has grown heavier, yet lighter,
Reminding me that I am still a warrior, a fighter.

The box of ego is the one that bothers me the most,
Why does it house so many? Who do they host?

This box has those I need no more;
This is the one that will be emptied and I will let go.

The box of vulnerability is the one I wear;
This is the box that allows me to dare.

This box is the one that I continue to own.
Staying authentic, it's how I have grown.

The box of love that surrounds,
That's the box I will also keep, but still out of bounds.

This box has access to only a few,
Those who are true, both old and new.

The only other box that finds no place,
Is that of fakes. That I will replace.

This box will have the real and the true,
Cherished and welcomed, as there are only a few.

These boxes all carry a tale
Of freshness, of newness and that which is stale.

There will be some more boxes, I know.
Let the year begin and see how we go.

# COME, JUDGE ME

Oh, so you judged me?
And to what degree!

Did you not see
The scars from me judging me?

So please feel free
To take those words of decree.

My judgement of me, you see,
Has already made me beautifully me.

# 3 A.M. THOUGHTS

Three in the morning and sleep says bye.
You finally get off your bed with a loud, long sigh.

You think of the things you never should do;
Three in the morning, even ghosts don't move.

You make a cup of coffee and then let the coffee make you,
You smile through the thoughts, and then you sigh out a few.

You find yourself wanting to calm your chaotic mind.
Then you say a prayer of gratitude for life has been kind.

When a thought escapes your soft heart, of the moments gone by,
You repackage those thoughts and you promise to
never let them die.

Then when you try hard not to think of those thoughts of pain,
You re-bin them in that trash bin and
hope it washes with the rain.

When loving thoughts come visiting you in the calm of the night,
You hold on to them like dear life, you just don't put up a fight.

Then when all seems to settle as coffee plays its role,
You finally wake up fully and start hugging your soul.

It's ok to have chaos sometimes in your mind.
Let it brew around for a bit, but let it not grind.

Hold on to the thoughts and continue to let them be.
Tell them to let you love you and not kill you softly.

# MOMENTARY INSANITY

They drifted, the pieces meant for me,
Into the alleys of your momentary insanity.

Deep gashes and open wounds left to see,
In a presence of uncertainty.

Each piece, a lesson it shared,
The sad nothingness of the soul bared.

What was mine would now never be,
Lost in the throngs of deep sea.

Trust, commitment and faith shaken,
Empty words of happiness now taken.

Wounds they remain open to heal,
My soul, once bared, now has a seal.

Peace, happiness, acceptance, those pieces I need.
My wounded heart and hurtful soul I feed.

They drifted—those pieces meant for me,
In the dark alleys of your momentary insanity.

# STORIES TUBED

Sitting on the tube this morning, I thought,
These people in here, how many battles have they fought?

What stories do they carry inside them all?
What has left them looking forlorn, yet standing tall?

That man out there, with his nice suit and tie,
What are his secrets? Is his life a truth or a lie?

That young girl standing by the door,
Who made advances at her which she had to ignore?

That old man, with his tired eyes and droopy stance,
Why does he look away every time we glance?

That woman dressed up to her core,
What makes her lips quiver as she looks at the floor?

That little boy jumping up and down,
How long before this world will take away his sound?

Watching them, stories unfold in my mind,
Leaving me more determined to be non-judgmental and kind.

# THE LOVE TIDE

Quietly, eyes closed, in a solitary tide,
Reaching inwardly, pondering over life's ride,

A simple truth chances upon the mind,
Hold on to moments, when love you find.

All else will come and go; leave it behind,
When you meet love, smile and be kind.

Life is promised fully to some, not to all,
Love is promised to all; accept and stand tall.

Eyes opened, joy and laughter added to the ride,
Love with openness, no need to hide.

# WHEN YOU ARE RIGHT AND WRONG

Things will go right and wrong;
Just keep playing your favourite song.

Embrace the wrong, smile at the right,
Laugh at the mistakes, never give up the fight.

Sit in a corner; ask the wrong why it felt so,
Are you really wrong just because someone said so?

Smile at her; the wrong needs that from you,
She will be hurting, wondering what to do.

When the wrong feels that it's right to be wrong,
Break away and start humming that song.

Then sit with the right and ask her why,
What makes her think that her right means the sky?

Perhaps she doesn't know that is there no wrong and no right,
It is what it is, try as you might.

Right and wrong are all perspectives of some kind,
Each a word, a meaning, a play of the mind.

# FOREVER KIND

Making my way to the four-poster bed,
Embracing the silence of the words unsaid,

Pondering on that which life doesn't let us see,
Just how many breaths are still left within me.

What if tomorrow is not promised and life eludes me?
Will life show me respect? How will it be?

Was my life lived purposefully, as promised to all?
Or did I rise so high within that I never saw the fall?

Did I live a life of truth even when there were lies around?
Or was it all just an illusion: the emptiness,
the fullness, the sound?

Did I love those who mattered, or whom I mattered to?
Would it matter if the ones who really matter are only a few?

Did I fulfil my purpose to the ones who chose my loving bosom?
Did I let them live and grow fully? Did I let them blossom?

To the ones who loved me as one should be loved,
Did I show them the respect their love deserved?

To the ones who hurt without thinking of my soul,
Did I let them fulfil their karma bank and leave no gaping hole?

To the ones who always brought out the best in me,
Did I ever graciously acknowledge gratitude and let them see?

To the one whose bosom I chose as my path to this life,
Was I kind to her? Did my love make her shine and
not give her strife?

Such thoughts keep lingering in my mind,
Intentions making their way to me to be forever kind.

So many questions, no answers yet to be,
And one truth—there is no promised tomorrow,
not for you, nor for me.

# 3 A.M. DIALOGUE WITH THOUGHTS

3 a.m. knocked again;
Sleep seemed to be in vain.

Thoughts came in through the door,
Some hanging out on the floor.

What's on your mind, a kind thought asked,
Just life, watching it go, at times masked.

Why the mask when life is so kind?
It's life. With this mask on, you'd be surprised what I find.

I find the dark truth of those who hide in a lie,
I find hidden truths of the moments gone by.

Truths and lies are both two sides of life,
One holding a candle, one holding a knife.

Ah, said the thought, I see your point,
Stay half masked, in this world disjoint.

But don't let this world get to you,
Stay unmasked, at least with a few.

Those that matter will never speak a lie;
Live your truth with them until your last goodbye.

# PILL FOR LIFE

Off fell the duvet this morning,
As the feet hit the floor.

A voice smiling over the shower, crooning,
continued as she ran through the door.

Morning coffee and a pill she popped,
In a flash, those moments were deleted and stopped.

A spring in her step, a song on her lips,
Music inside, swaying her hips.

A pocketful of pills she had found,
Carefully selected and shared around.

A pink pill to find the joy in small things,
A green pill to let go of the insecurity and stings,

A red pill to keep the danger at bay,
A blue pill to make that beautiful love stay,

A yellow pill when one felt jaundiced inside,
A purple pill to keep that outer garbage outside,

A black pill rarely used, but always kept on standby,
For that moment when it's time to say goodbye.

# WHEN THE MIRROR SPOKE

Peeping at the image in front,
She couldn't help but double up and grunt.

She stared back, surprise on her face;
Was this person going grey with grace?

She asked the mirror what she thought,
The mirror said, "Well, let's see what you've got".

I see those eyes with wrinkles around,
Carrying pieces of ups and downs.

And those lips and that crooked smile!
Ah, joy and laughter still visit once in a while.

Then that crinkly nose: what happened to thee?
It still carries the smell of egos that you won't set free.

And those cheeks: did they lose their high bone?
Remember when your glasses were coloured? They too shone.

Ah, now those lines, mapped on the face,
My love, it's the stories, chapters leaving their trace.

The mirror said that the stranger staring back at me,
Isn't a stranger. This person is free.

The stories she carried are novels bound,
A library of memoirs, she found.

Every word was etched in a line or two,
Some crafted and shining in those strands too.

And, said the mirror, those little grey strands that you see,
Are a library of life, an undocumented, unlabelled tree.

Ah, said the mirror to the face, "Stop staring and walk along".
Go on. Go forth. Life is a blessed bitch. You stay strong".

# REAL TRUTH

My truth you don't hear,
So I will give you my lie.

You ask me, "How are you, dear?"
I say "I am good" as inside, I die.

My truth is not your reality, you say,
So I can only accept the goodbye.

I feel incredulous when you ask me why,
I walk away, I despair.
I sigh.
But, I don't cry.

# SHE WALKED

With a spring in her step,
She opened the door of her street.
She walked.
She talked.

A prayer on her lips,
Wading through the skips,
She walked.
She talked.

The person inside had grown this year;
There was more joy, less fear.

The silence of the words had found their voice,
In the bustling energy, she felt no noise.

Lessons received. Some learnt. Some unlearnt,
Happiness captured. Negatives burnt.

Gratefulness. Acceptance humbly allowed,
Forgiving some. Letting go of some. With head bowed.

Time respected. Each breath was a blessing in sight,
Each day fully lived. Welcoming day after night.

Love allowed. Through a small peephole,
Watching, observing each play their role.

She had woken up and the sun was shining through,
Today, loving herself, she had found her love too.

# SELFISH

It was a cold, dark day in Mumbai. It was just another day for everyone, especially for the little girl. She was going to have a hungry day. She was only six years old. She had learnt to observe little signs just from watching her mother and her siblings. It was day three she counted. No smell of coffee being made in the morning. This morning her frail little body with impish eyes and soft face looked frailer.

Oh, how she loved it when she saw her mother sitting by the kerosene stove each morning in the smallest of rooms that was her whole world. She watched her beautiful mother – her soft face was sullen from hunger and sadness. She loved watching her mother do things around the house in her sari. The same sari every day that was washed at night and worn again the next morning. The little girl watched as the stove was pumped a few times, the match lit and the aluminium kettle put on the stove with two cups of water and two cubes of coffee. Then the waiting, the kettle whistled for a bit and then her mother knew exactly what to do. She would turn the stove off then pour dark strong coffee into the four cups, add some milk and give each of the three siblings a piece of bread that she would cook on the pan. On some special days, the bread would be heated with some oil. That taste was always lingering. Most days it was simple bread and coffee and that was good enough. That would be the highlight of the morning – little siblings and big smiles.

On this day, there was no kettle; no coffee aroma and no smiles, just like the previous two days. The siblings had to go to school. Hungry. She would be dropped off at the neighbour's house and had to wait until mother returned from work to get some food.

That evening all three siblings waited eagerly. Their tummies were beyond rumbling; they were hurting. Hunger caused deep pain, she knew and she had been in pain for so long now.

Mother arrived from work looking very sad and dejected. The little ones knew that this was going to be another painful night. She watched mother sitting by the stove as all three of them huddled next to her, trying to smile. Mother tried hard to get the kettle going but the stove needed kerosene to start and there wasn't any. Then she took a piece of bread from her bag, one small slice of bread which looked hard. The little girl looked around at the faces, all just staring at the piece of bread. No pan on the stove this time and the bread had to be eaten as it was. She watched her mother dividing the bread into three parts. In a voice that had no strength left, she said, "I have had a bite on my way here, so this is for my babies. Eat."

Immediately, the little girl heard her oldest sibling who was eight years her senior, say "Ah, I was so lucky today. Raja's mother shared some food with me earlier. So I am full".

The little girl knew he was lying. She knew her brother always shared whenever he got anything, even if it was the tiniest piece of something. The other sibling, who was sickly from leading such a dysfunctional life, hardly spoke. But now she said in a quiet voice,

"I have a tummy ache. I cannot eat".

The mother looked at the piece and the little girl. She said gently, "Here, it is all yours." The little girl looked at them all and knew all were lying. She knew they wanted her to have that small piece so she would not have to go hungry another night.

She didn't know what to do. She sat there in silence with tears rolling down her cheeks as she so wanted her family to share that piece. She took it and slowly started chewing on to the hard bread until there was none left. She got up and sat on the side of their tiny bed, feeling strangely sad.

Inside her soul she recognised the pain of doing something that wasn't what she truly wanted. She wanted to share but she didn't know what she was meant to do. She had no control over what happened that evening, as she was too little to have a voice.

**She was labelled selfish from that day on. That label stuck.**

# THE LITTLE GIRL

That little girl, nearly giving up on her life,
In her hand, was a shiny bladed knife.

Pretending not to know or understand,
I sat next to her, as I gently held her hand.

"Little girl, what's troubling you my doll?",
"Why these stooped shoulders, when you normally stand tall"?

"I have nothing that I can understand nor can I share,
My thoughts, my fears, they don't get me, they don't care.

Sleep seems to be what my mind craves, day and night,
I can't seem to fight this darkness, I can't see the light.

I go to sleep each night, thinking tomorrow will be a better day,
Yet, morning arrives and the deep dark thoughts
make me their prey.

Each day I barely manage to make myself stay alive,
What's the point of this living, if I can't feel this life?"

I held her hand tighter and gently held her to me,
I knew she needed just that love and for me to let her be.

I knew the struggles that little girl must feel,
In this world with laughter, such pain she must deal.

All I could do, was gently hold her and say,
"Little girl, you are safe, hold on and live another day".

# EYES THAT CANNOT SEE

Sitting with her, watching with my eyes,
Talking to a sightless girl, I was full of sighs.

So many questions tumbled out, words on top of me,
What did she see, how did she dream,
when colours she couldn't see?

"What colour is the colour of ego?" she asked me,
"That's the colour I don't need sight for; my soul can see.

"That mask that is put up when fear walks in through the door,
I don't need to see that mask,
I only sense the sound of fear on the floor.

"That face of insecurity, that you all have to meet,
That emotion stays away, at times only at my feet.

"Those faces that you see, at times one with two,
Do you really think I need sight? To that, I say boo.

"I dream of things that make me smile with the senses
that live in me;

I thank the universe for its kindness and the terrors I don't see.

"I worry most for those who have sight, yet cannot see,
All they do is shut their souls and pretend not to be.

"I mostly fear those that watch the unheard pain;
They shut their hearts to their senses, all for their own gain.

"In this world of sighted blind, I see through my sightless eyes,
Eyes that have the power. They watch and live the painful lies.

# STANDING STRONG

She stood before the mirror; shockingly, I saw,
Frowning, squirming, falling, tightening my jaw.

Searching through my ammo case, I held a sharp one in hand,
Ready for the war, fingers walking through the neck land.

One big, white, grey strand stood teasingly away;
Oh, I was all ready to cut it loose and not let it stay.

She put up a fight; honestly, what more can I say? With all her
dark mates cheering us, she was the lone grey.

I could hear the claps from those watching us play;
When she let go, that grey strand made my day.

Holding her between my fingers,
I watched in wonderment as I lay,

One little strand and such a lesson! How to repay?

She taught me that no one will be spared,
What we have today won't be as we once cared.

Black will turn white, and white will turn grey;
A legacy of love, kindness, humbleness, that's all that will stay.

# GAOL (PRISON)

It's dark and there's nowhere to go,
Step up, all say, go with the flow.

I try hard and put on a face,
Then I fall flat; I bring disgrace.

I run inside myself; I try to hide,
Endless helpless moments I have cried.

It gets darker each passing day,
I wake up, as I look for that shining ray.

I get back into that comfortable duvet,
But that doesn't help my thoughts not to stray.

You need help, my soul screams at me,
This darkness, please, can you just let me be.

I fight, constantly, with myself, with the demons inside,
I'm scared to lose all I have, including my pride.

Please wake me up from this dark nightmare,
Oh no, don't wake up me, this pain I can't bear.

These two parts of me gnaw at my soul,
I need freedom, I want light, I want out from this role.

# SEPARATED FROM ME

Separating myself from that part of me,
I disconnected the connection from that ecstasy.

No longer carrying that part of my heart,
That flamed the desire, got the fire to start.

No longer carrying that infinite longing inside,
The day that match was lit, I slowly died.

When death came, I could no longer hide,
Feelings shut down and even words left my side.

Once, there was a reason for the bounce in the soul,
But everything changed. That twin love was no longer my goal.

Feeling separated from self has its own impact,
I smile, I laugh, I exist. And just survive. At times, I act.

No longer will the soul meet that soul again,
The twin souls will no longer share that pain.

Separated from self, the soul did compromise,
Now it lives in its acceptance, life the guise.

# IT'S ALL TEMPORARY

That little man came up to me,
Eyes filled with pain for all to see,

A terrified look of desperation in sunken eyes,
A smile hidden but ready to escape and disguise.

A dark cloud had cast a darker shadow in his soul;
The depth of his despair was bigger than that hole.

I held his hand and looked into his simmering heart;
I heard the sound of brokenness, his pieces falling apart.

One by one, together, silently, we picked them all,
Some we put back slowly, as some were continuing to fall.

"It's ok, little man," said my voice to his brokenness.
"Pick up these pieces, let go of chaos and find your stillness."

The broken pieces will repair and bring a new you,
This heart will grow beautifully, will repair and renew.

What is now needed is for you to clearly see
That this brokenness, this darkness is all temporary.

That light around you, keep it burning inside;
The switch is in your hands, put on that light,
set the darkness aside.

# THE DANCING STORM

The stars and the moon were dancing in the dark night,
Upwardly, heavenly, swaying to the music. Oh, what a sight!

Their sparkle had found their way into my well;
They glittered brighter than the stars where I dwell.

The moon had put on her best show so far,
She got gasps from the wind, the clouds,
and even that evening star.

All were in their glory, dancing their dance,
Each one lovingly, shyly stealing a glance.

Then in a flash; it all seemed to change,
The dark monsters had arrived, to destroy all in their range.

Along came the wind, trying to claim its place,
It stormed through the celebrations, leaving its destructive trace.

Then came the cloud, trying to one up the storm,
The beautiful moon, the dizzy stars wondered where it was from.

That evening star just looked at the stars and wept,
She wanted nothing from this havoc and nothing was left.

One by one, the stars collided and they seem to lose their way,
The moon was adamant; it was her night,
and she was here to stay.

She held her head high and shone her light of gold;
The wind, the storm, their darkness, they could no longer hold.

The moon and her stars in their splendour put on all their light,
They brought back their colours and danced away
through the night.

My well had seen the light, the dark and the storm prance,
With relief, it settled finally and joined in that moon dance.

# CANDLES FOR CHRISTMAS

As I lit the candles next to the tree,
One for each one, no more with me,

The tree felt the light from the candles galore,
And you stayed with us, although you were no more.

So this Christmas, let's keep them in mind;
Through our good deeds, let's continue to be kind.

Some have love, some loves have gone;
Let's be mindful for those who are forlorn.

Let's start with this Christmas; light a candle or more,
Let the light keep shining; let their memories grow.

# GRATITUDE AND LOYALTY

The little girl knew something was not right. All her friends' dads went to work. The mothers stayed at home and looked after them. In her case, the mother left early morning each day and the father slept all day, speaking incoherently at times. He was a good dad though and when awake he took the little girl everywhere with him.

She looked around the little place they called home, it was tiny; her mother had managed to fit the smallest of beds into that place. That bed had her dad's presence. The three siblings slept under the bed whilst the parents slept above. Some days, if she was lucky; especially when she had a fever she would get to sleep close to mother on the bed, alongside her. Those were the best nights for her, feeling her mother's breath on her.

To date the memory of that breath helps her sleep on nights when sleep evades.

The home had a steel cupboard, a small corner for kitchen utensils mostly arranged on the shelf neatly and the stove at the bottom with some other utensils that were used for day-to-day cooking. The bed was on one side of the room. There was a small bath area behind the bed; it was open with some water pots to cover the area if someone was lucky enough to take a bucket shower. There was no water tap in the house; water was brought in every morning from the neighbourhood communal tap at hours that the little girl had no idea about. Mother used to do all of that as she was her magical mama. Mother did everything, magically.

Every morning and through the afternoon her dad would sleep. The little girl would be trapped in the house, locked in with the drunken dad. Too little to even reach and unlock the latch of the door and escape for a bit, she learnt to live in her head. She made up stories and sang the songs that played on the little transistor radio all day. That habit would live with her forever.

Every evening her dad would take her to a filthy side shop that sold illicit liquor. There were dark blue barrels everywhere and benches that had no seats on them. The men who came there looked hungry, angry and drunk. She never understood why they smelled so much and why they shouted all the time. Those were great moments for that little girl, simply because she got to sit next to her father and hold his hand. He hardly spoke but he was present. He was awake and he was her Da, she loved him to bits in those moments.

Now, if you asked her what he sounded like she wouldn't be able to tell you as all she remembered were his starched white shirts and pants. He was well dressed even to visit the illicit liquor place. Her Da was like that, he dressed up.

As much as she loved her Da, she hated being there. Her only solace was her loyal Bruno, a little street dog who had adopted the family and would follow Da and the little girl around. Bruno hardly ever left her side.

Da getting drunk with his buddies, sitting by his side and Bruno at her feet, the little girl felt most safe in those moments.

Then one day something horrible happened during an evening like this. Da, Bruno, the little girl at the illicit liquor shop with the drunk buddies – all there, as usual.

The little girl saw a blue van with big, fat, potbellied men holding batons in their hands pull up at the shop. Those uniformed men hit everyone in sight and dragged them all into the blue van. The little girl was pushed into this milieu of sticks, vomit, shouting, beating and noise. It all happened so suddenly and so fast. Before she knew it she was bundled into this van that had grills and she couldn't see outside. As the van pulled out of that place she realised she had lost Bruno. She felt fear. She screamed and cried. She got a slap from a drunk angry man for being so noisy. Da slapped that man and that was it, screams and shouting continued.

She remembered being thrown into a small room with hundreds of men. She was on her Da's shoulders by then and he could hardly stand. She still didn't know where Bruno was.

That night was horrible. All she wanted was to go home and be with her mother and her siblings. All she could see were dirty old men shouting at each other; some were vomiting. That noise and smell stayed with the little girl forever.

Then something happened. Da's name was called and the little girl along with her Da went out to the front desk at the police station.

She saw the one person who was her entire world - her mother, standing there. Simple, strong, resigned. The little girl wondered what her mother had sold this time to bail her Da out. Another tumbler from the house? Her last bangle?

They walked back home with Bruno following. Bruno had found her.

The little girl heard noises that night. She knew Da had to show his love to her mother for bailing him out. She could hear her mother's screams and cries. The little girl wondered what it was about people that they hurt the ones who love them the most. Was it shame, was it guilt that Da felt that night that he needed to hide away from?

**That night, the little girl learnt about gratitude.**

**She also learnt about loyalty. Bruno was always there for her, licking her face. She learnt that animals loved unconditionally.**

# IF I WAS HAPPINESS

It's been a hard day,
With no words left to say.

With nothing going right,
You want to give up the fight.

Then you see someone you know,
And it's not your stresses you want to show.

You fake your face with a smile.
Showing sadness—it's just not your style.

Who put these pressures on you?
Why put happiness so above you?

To pretend that life is bright?
When it doesn't feel right?

Imagine happiness and the pressures it must feel.
If happiness was one of us and had so much to deal.

What would happiness do if she didn't feel right?
Would she be herself or fight darkness with her might?

What a huge responsibility to always give its light.
Let happiness be okay when life loses sight.

So when you meet someone, when life feels like night,
Allow yourself to say, "It's ok, I am not alright."

# WALK WITH ME

You walk down the street,
With eyes wide open.
You just walk and you follow your feet,
Feeling the breeze and feeling the sun.

Where will they take you?
Have you ever let yourself see?
Will they take you to places they knew?
Will they take you to your destiny?

Today I walked that path unknowingly,
My feet carrying me to places I couldn't see.
Then it just happened; it flowed glowingly.
My feet had taken me on a new journey.

A shining light had appeared in sight.
Was I going to allow it or would I put up a fight?

These feet: should I let them be?
Allow them, step by step, to places I cannot yet see?

These feet have walked past rubble and sand,
They've walked into oases of emotions and pain not grand,

These feet have also walked away from the thorny kind,
Those who appear to smile with a soul you cannot find.

These feet have also walked on fires and survived the burn,
These feet, these burnt feet, what have they learnt?

Stop, I say. Turn around and walk the other way.
Stay in that place where only happiness can stay.

Hearing this, the feet look up and smile at me.
They say, "Love, walk with me, trust me. I will be your journey."

# MASKED

Deep laughter of a special kind,
Twinkle in her eyes, where did she find?

Happiness shining within her soul,
Energetic chatter, hugs galore.

Spreading warmth, sharing smiles,
Pouring positivity, walking miles.

Are you for real? she was asked.
Is she? Or she is just beautifully masked?

# PIECES, PISCES, PEACE, RETURNS

When times are tough in life,
And you just can't see the light,

You try to find peace, and all you see is strife,
You seek the sun, but only darkness is in sight.

Close your eyes and look within,
Reach for your madness; pull up your chin.

You are a warrior; let yourself know,
Spread your strength wherever you go.

# VOICES NOT HEARD

Little big voices,
Voices with noises,
Noises of screams,
Screams of scrambling,
Scrambling to come out,
Come out to punch a few,
A few lines of thoughts,
Thoughts that come and go,
Go into the little big world,
A world that hears no more.

# DARKNESS

If you weren't here,
Where would I be?
Asked my darkness,
To me.

There would be no songs,
No music from rights and wrongs,
No poetry to sing of my woes,
Nor stories written in awkward prose.

If you weren't here,
I wouldn't be,
Said that little voice
From inside of me.

# LIFE WILL TEACH US

Deafening noise
Of silence.

Deep heaviness
Of emptiness.

Dark loneliness
Of crowds.

# FEAR

---

"Where is he, where is he?" Loud noises and knocks on the door could be heard waking the little girl from her fantasy. She froze.

Here she was lying as usual, next to her Da. Of course, she had no idea that he was drunk. This is how dads were, she thought. Her Da slept all day and only got up to eat and drink that smelly liquid. When mother returned home, there would be loud noises, cries, perhaps his way of demonstrating his love for her.

She could hear that door being pushed. Da was not moving as she tried to wake him up. She tried to hide under the sheets. She wanted the noises to stop. She could smell something – fear. That was the smell. It was dark, disturbing, violent and alone, it made you feel sick in the stomach and it made you want to throw up. That little girl felt that and more.

She quickly left her Da's side and hid under the bed. Just as she managed to squeeze herself into a ball in the farthest corner of the bed, the door sprung open. She could see many feet with different types of footwear, pushing in. There were loud sounds of violence, she could even see a large shiny blade. Fear had completely taken over. She had no idea what to do nor what would happen next.

All she could hear was the words the men uttered. "Scoundrel, useless, borrowing money and sleeping it off, bloody drunk." They had come to get him. But he wouldn't move. The little girl was shaking under the bed. She wanted her Da to be safe.

Finally, the little girl decided that she was going to help save her dad. She came out of hiding. She felt all eyes suddenly fixed on her. There was silence. She could feel the noise of the silence. The water from the little pot in the corner went "tap, tap, tap." The noise of the silence was stronger than the noises she had heard earlier, she realised.

She went up to the one who was holding the shiny blade. Their eyes met - his dark black from anger, hers dark brown and wide with fear. They shared a silent conversation between them. In that moment, the little girl felt she was reading a book, the entire story was being unfolded in his eyes. His dark black eyes started getting clearer and softer.

He took the little girl's hand and in a strong voice she heard him say, "Okay everyone, let's go."

And off they went, leaving the door open, Da still in bed, oblivious to the fear that had just entered the little girl's life.

**That day, the little girl learnt the smell of fear and forgiveness.**

# WHEN FEAR MET HOPE

Have you ever felt a fear so deep,
It takes with it all the joy and happiness you reap?

Sweat pores down your brows like blood,
Seeping its way into your dreams, pouring in flood.

It's deep, it's dark, it smells of ice;
It scares the daylights out of you, nothing seems nice.

The nightmares soon arrive, taking away the light;
Day turns dark and it feels like a forever kind of night.

That fear, that scary thing, where does it rest,
When all you want is to be calm and you are doing your best?

It falls around you like a shadow in the dark,
Covers you up, walks with you, leaving it's mark.

Yes, that's the fear that even fear fears;
It's the kind of fear that runs on ten gears.

That's the fear one feels as these words I write,
What does one do, when that's all there is in sight?

Does one push away the fear and allow the hope to stay?
Will the hope be stronger when everything feels so grey?

Let's see who wins the challenge: the fear or the hope.
Maybe the fear needs a kick, so it is left with no scope.

Perhaps the hope will come through, bringing with it its light;
Maybe this hope is that hope; this hope will set it right.

# ONE DAY

Eyes closed,
The noise won't kill.
The chaotic soul
Will stay still.

When it crawls,
Through memory lane,
It will allow forgiveness,
To seep through the pain.

The ice will melt;
Only love with stay.
The fire of warm love
Will return one day.

# STORIES INSIDE

Memories must have memories,
Stories within stories.

Stories written and forgotten, or so you think.
The stories get told, tiny drops at times, as a blink.

Nothing goes; it stays within,
Memories, hold on to them with a grin.

That yesterday carries stories of its own;
Look back only to know how you have grown.

Memories, they do have memories, I know,
Let them stay; nurture them as you grow.

# BUBBLE WRAP ME

Sighing softly,
Walking home,
Seeking comfort,
I find you,
My bubble wrap.

You keep me safe,
From the hardness,
The darkness,
And the toxins
In my space.

I shall stay wrapped
In you,
Through the year,
Until I find that peace,
And feel no fear.

# JUST BE

She asked, "What is it that you wish for me?"
"I wish you love, laughter and strength to just be,
To live in a world that sometimes cannot see,
It locks you up within and asks you to be free.

"It will put you in shackles and hold you imprisoned;
It will make you look within, as if you have sinned.
It will put you in chains and want you to plot your own escape,
Just remember, just be and just feel safe.

"It will ask things of you that you could ever imagine;
Think, feel, cry if you must and do it with a grin.
Break the shackles that are tied around that soul so true;
Live your life fully and freely, that's my only advice for you."

# DREAMT OF ME

Dreamt of me last night,
Dead, alive, it was a sight.
The box looked heavy but bright,
Looked like I had gone without a fight.

Then I saw someone at the door,
Said, "Hey, you can't be here no more.
Hold my hand, let me show you the shore,
You have so much in store."

I remember waking up and opening the lid,
I took a giant step and halfway, I slid.
No more detractors shall see me hid,
All the darkness, I had farewell bid.

This dream with its vividness and its story,
Let me bask in its world and its glory.

I am now awakened with a story to tell,
No more goodbyes, not yet farewell.

# 3 DOORS

There are three doors, as I see,
That allow one to let go or let it be.

One door remains fully open
For recreation, laughter, and fun.

In it, there will be no surprise;
It leads to rooms of joy and loving cries.

Friendships, naughtiness, and madness are packed,
Bitterness, insecurities, and negatives all sacked.

Then there is that door which is slightly ajar,
You can check in the baggage from afar.

It allows room for laughter as well as tears;
It contains insecurities and life's fears.

It houses those who have left an impact,
Leaving their footprints with their selfless act.

Then that door that you see in the middle of the room?
It's where there are skeletons, with all its gloom.

This door remains locked, still in sight,
For those who have brought in conflict and fight.

This door is the one that has been sealed,
The content in it can never be healed.

This door is the one that lives in a lock,
It contains the remains of things out of stock.

The three doors are all passages of life,
To be used for love, for dreams, and for strife.

# VOICES INSIDE

Inside us lives that voice,
Ours, theirs, perhaps by choice,

Using words that carry truth and lies,
Those of happiness and painful cries,

Guarding us from an untruthful mask,
Cautioning us before unsealing becomes a task.

Voices carry words of no use;
Words are words—some, a form of abuse.

Much has been said and many half truths
By living souls, all half crooks.

That voice carries more than just a sound;
It carries with it their lies, square and round.

Voices. Voices. Voices. Inside and outside.
Should we hold on and take them in our stride?

There is another voice talking to us,
Asking, begging us to set it free. It's so rough.

That voice, it needs to go,
It's rubbish. All rubbish. Just throw.

Keep only the voice that shows you the way,
To make mindful choices and never to sway.

Keep that voice that allows you to see,
the fake, the real, and the rubbish with clarity.

# KNOCKING ON OUR DOOR

Death came knocking several times, not long ago;
Once it came very close as it washed to the shore.

Pushing it away, the door was shut tight;
The darkness gave way to light.

That death wasn't the only death though;
The death we face every day, where does that show?

Like warriors, we keep smiling through it all;
How many times it kills us, yet we stand tall.

Until one day we say, "No more.
Stay if you wish; we won't go."

Life will be lived today and tomorrow;
Death, that everyday death, show her the door.

# STRANGERS

---

The little girl was beyond excited today, her siblings were taking her out to the movies. This was the first time she would be watching a real movie on the big screen. All these years, she had been watching movies through the stories shared by her siblings, particularly her sister. There were certain movies she had watched only through her sister's eyes and to date even if she heard the songs from those movies, or watched snippets of them, she remembered all the scenes. That was how her sister shared the stories and how the little girl listened fully. Every word was taken in. Perhaps this was how she learnt to be a storyteller herself?

This day was special and was always going to be special. She had been dressed in her Sunday best. Her brother had taken extra effort to tie her hair up in two ponytails, with beautiful red ribbons, just as she liked it. Her floral green dress was the one she always wore when she went out, the only one she had, which had been handed down to her through her sister, who had in turn been given it from a distant cousin. Today she didn't care. She felt pretty. She felt happy.

To date, she still remembers the feel of the theatre, the seats, the people around and that large screen with those people wearing thick makeup. All that she had only heard so far, she could now see. She was in heaven.

She enjoyed the movie. She remembered the whistles, the clapping and the crowd. She had never sat on a chair before. The theatre seat was so amazing, she thought. She didn't want to leave when the movie ended. The siblings had to drag her out.

Holding her siblings' hands, she walked out, waiting to go home and re-live the entire experience. She couldn't wait to share this with her Ma, who had been unable to make it that day due to work.

As they stepped out, they realised that it had been pouring relentlessly all that time they were watching the movie. So much so that the roads had clogged up with water, which was now waist-high. It felt scary.

The three siblings were little and alone; everything seemed so dark and unreal. The little girl held her siblings' hands tighter as thunder roared above. She remembered her mother's fears of thunder and lightning. On days like this the mother would kneel down and start praying, and all the siblings would kneel beside her.

The siblings decided to run on to the road and start walking towards home. Home was far away and wading through the water was a huge challenge. Suddenly the BEST bus (local Bombay bus) pulled up next to them. Without any thought other than the desire to protect his little sisters, the brother pushed them gently into the bus. The siblings needed to get off in two stops, and then home was over the bridge on the other side, a long-distance away. The three of them headed inside the already overcrowded bus, the siblings still holding on to the little girl's hand.

Suddenly, the little girl heard loud sounds and angry voices. She looked up in fear. The conductor (the ticket collector) had just slapped her brother and was calling him names. The brother had offered some change to the conductor and apparently that wasn't enough for the tickets. So the conductor decided he was going to share a moral lesson that day and shouted at the top of his voice about poor urchins who took buses without being able to afford them. They should simply be walking through the rainwater as was their class, he exclaimed and buses were for those who could afford them he added and shared with all those who were willing to listen.

In this way the three siblings were being harassed. The shouting and the unkind words were now intense and came from all corners of the bus. Even those who had no idea what the commotion was about, joined in.

It is interesting how mobs work. They may not know what is going on and they may not be interested either. They just want to participate in the drama and create further drama. The same thing happened that afternoon.

But the noises stopped just as abruptly. The little girl heard a stranger give money to the conductor. "Take this please," he said, "And don't harass the little children. They seem to be from a decent, educated family". That was it. That stopped the mob from venting their frustration further.

The brother was reluctant to take the money from a complete stranger. The stranger looked very kind. The two sisters looked very scared, compelling the brother to make the decision to accept the stranger's help.

To date, the bus incident remains a story that is bigger than the movie and is a reminder of many things.

**That day, the little girl learnt a few lessons: most people don't care. They will kick you when you are down, but there will be one person who will care, and that is enough. Strangers are sometimes kinder than your own.**

# BIG BANG SOUL

Bang, said the soul, just as I breathed my first,
Pieces of me scattered around the earth.

Every one on my journey got a piece of me,
That piece of my soul that no one could see

In the nod of the head, in the meeting of the eyes,
Creating love, laughter and all those cries.

All were just parts of me, coming to say hi;
I have been welcoming you all, knowing the soul doesn't lie.

I looked for that biggest part of me that is still out there;
The one who will have it, I know will care.

Then it arrived silently, that loud, big bang,
My heart melted, birds chirped and my soul truly sang.

Recognition happened within a moment of time,
The heart, the body, the soul all in rhyme.

This piece had reconnected with the biggest part of me;
Two big pieces coming together, how strong can it be?

Only time will show the power of these souls,
No room for labels, no expectations, purity playing its role.

Let these pieces find their joy through it all;
I kneel, I pray, let these pieces rise always, never to fall.

# GAME OF SHAME

Me,
They tried to tame,
To defame,
To shame.
Ah, I was game.

Chuckling,
I played along,
Whistled to their song,
Right or wrong,
But stayed strong.

Smiling,
Promises made,
Of white, grey, shade,
Aware, unafraid,
Bare soul, I laid.

Painfully,
Every cell exposed,
In over triple doze,

Soul froze.
That's how it goes.

Finally,
They let go,
Taming, shaming, defaming no more.

Change happened like never before.
The game had become a bore.
They pushed me no more.

# MAGIC OF LIFE

It was a warm winter of madness and sin,
It was cold outside but warm within.

Yes, you read that right,
Light, dark, hot, cold—it was truly a sight.

Through the coldness, the warmth arose,
Basking in the sun even when the ice froze.

Perhaps magic had shown its magical face,
When your feet walked in a mindless haze.

When tears only mean tears of joy,
When laughter shared left you all coy,

When the chirping birds only meant one thing,
That this was totally real, not a fling,

When the passing clouds talked to you, The rain that followed
arried the magic through.

When the flutter in your heart carried a spark,
That which would light a billion hearts, so far dark,

Then you open your eyes and look around,
But nothing seems as magical as it sounds.

The winter is cold; let's get that straight,
The warmth of the summer stays until late.

That's when you wake up to the reality of life,
You ask: is life magical, with all its strife?

The magic is what magic is about.
It's only magic, without a doubt.

Magic is magical and will find its way,
For those who believe in it, it will stay.

The magic you create will spread far and wide,
Cold, warm, icy, dark—the real magic is inside.

# FRAGILE LOVE

Fragile
Is that which can break;
It's not the heart
That pulls you apart.

**Fragile**
Is that which can crush;
It's not the soul
That leaves a hole.

**Fragile**
Is that love
That can live and that can die?
Without a warning, can it say goodbye?

**Fragile**
Is that love,
That needs to be sealed,
Tendered, cared for and healed?

### Fragile
Is that love
That plays in the rain,
And holds you in its arms, despite the pain?

### Fragile
Is that love
That knows how to live?
That doesn't want anything, just wants to give?

### Fragile
Is that love
When times are tough?
Which warms up your soul, no matter how rough?

# LIGHT

In the billion points of darkness,
Be that one light.

Let the fire inside,
Engulf everyone in sight.

Let the smile,
Shine so very bright.

So that every dark thought,
Disappears into the night.

# LOVE AND TRUST

"I will love you forever, will you be mine, will you spend the rest of your life with me?" Those questions were proposed to the little girl at twenty-two. She was ecstatic. The love of her life had asked her to marry him. She had found her heaven.

Jumping with absolute joy, she said, "yes, yes!"

Preparations started for that big day. "Why waste time?" the family said. "They are both young, well settled and in love. Let's get them engaged quickly and within six months, let's get them married."

Six long months, she thought. But she agreed as six months can also just disappear in no time. So many preparations had to be managed in the meantime, as weddings are by no means a small affair.

A beautiful engagement ceremony was performed, love laughter, family, fun and a future to look forward to. The little girl felt like a princess with her handsome prince. He was handsome, well placed in an advertising agency. She was attractive and well placed in an agency as well. It seemed like it was a match made in heaven.

But she was so wrong. When things seem too good to be true, maybe that's when you know it isn't. You learn this from experiences, your own experiences.

Countdown to the wedding. A week left. 1993. Curfew in Mumbai, which meant that people had to be off the streets by 9 pm. The family was busy with wedding preparations and cards were being distributed in the chaos and stress of Mumbai of those days. There was always tension in the air.

The excitement of the wedding had seeped into the little girl, now a young woman as well. Her clothes shopping had started and she was getting her trousseau together. Every day was exciting and she had so much to look forward to.

Then one evening after work she decided to pay her fiancé a visit at his home. A quick visit before the curfew she thought. She had been informed that his family was out visiting someone, so it was a great opportunity for some alone time. Those were the days of no mobile phones, only landlines. The young girl wanted to surprise her future husband.

Her future in-laws had given her a spare key, which she had never used before. So, off she went, excited and looking forward to giving her fiancé a surprise. She unlocked the door quietly; tiptoeing she went into the house looking for him, smiling as she walked through the lounge, kitchen, room one, room two and room three - the bedroom. Suddenly, her smile froze. At that moment the entire world stood still for her and the blood from her entire being, drained. In that moment, she felt her world falling apart. The sound of a heart breaking is deep and painful and yet it has no sound, no blood.

The love of her life was with someone else, loving someone else, as she stood there, shocked. Heaven had shown her hell. She said nothing as she just stood there silently and in total disbelief. The mind and body were now not aligned; she wanted to say something but words would not come out.

The side lamp fell as she turned and the lovers were now looking at her, surprised. Ashamed, perhaps? perhaps not. They had the look of being caught for sure. That look, the little young woman would never forget.

No words were spoken. The room had gone quiet.

The young girl slowly made her way out. Shutting the door behind her that evening, much of what could have been was shut off. Life would never be the same again, she knew.

She ran, she ran over 20 km that day. Through the curfew, through the life that she had to leave behind. She ran and she ran.

She didn't stop running for years. Trust and love had become her biggest hell.

**The little young girl had now learnt that love can be heaven and it can be hell.**

**The little young girl knew that nothing was truly yours. Everything was temporary.**

# WHICH FACE IS MY FRIEND'S?

**(Part 1)**

---

Eyes smile, eyes laugh,
They say you can see the soul in the eyes;
I saw yours and trusted.

That face which shared my pain,
Held my hand and cried my tears.

Then the face changed;
The eyes smiled and laughed.

I still saw glimpses of the soul,
Sharing my pain,
And holding my hand.

This time, though, I clearly saw,
The shiny knife close to my heart,

Ready to stab as soon as my head turned,
As it perhaps may have.

Which face was my friend's?
I kept wondering and hurting

Until it all made sense within.
There was only ever one face,
Half soul, hidden in smiles and laughs.
It was fully hidden by lies lived in the soul,
And it carried a knife,
Covered in the trust of friendship,
Covered in the blood of a stabbed friend.

# WHICH FACE IS MY FRIEND'S?

### (Part 2)

They asked, "The truth, will you reveal
Of that friend who left you with nothing to feel?"

But then the question remains:
Is that a friend who leaves you in pain?

The ones who stab you in the back, smile, and pretend,
Can these ever be truly called friends?

Or that one who waits to see you smile,
Then stabs you with words, still smiling all the while?

Which face is my friend's? I have stopped to wonder now.
No more friends will stab me; that I won't allow.

# BUBBLE WRAPPED

The bubble wrapped soul slowly peeped out,
Breathing heavily, seemingly full of doubt.

Looked around, gazed into the endless ride,
Fearfully, nervously, it tried hard not to hide.

Hesitantly, it took it's first step towards the moon,
Such an indulgence was a curse, not a boon.

Opening the soul, showing such vulnerability,
Could one trust, did this soul have the ability?

Unsure, uncertain, it went back into it's bubble wrapped hole,
Let life be, let it unfold, screamed it's pieces
wanting to be whole.

# PEACE

---

You shut your eyes,
To stop the pain.

The heart bleeds,
Knowing it will happen again.

Praying for the world around,
When will peace be found?

# SHORT STORY

Here it is:
My short story.
Beautiful,
Sinful,
Sensuous,
Delightful,
Mysterious,
Magical,
Romantic,
And painful.
No, beyond painful.
A once upon a time
With no ending.
It is a story
With chapters to be written,
With words, passion, hurt,
Laughter,
Joy, euphoria,
And then more pain,

Suffering,
And some magic
Songs.
My story,
With a beginning,
And no ending.
Not yet.

# WHEN FAKE HAPPENS

Fake smiles shining through,
Slippery, pretending, but one knew.

Words used pretentiously, as they do,
Lying to themselves, forgetting others too.

Then the truth emerges so openly,
That what you knew is now exposed fully.

What do you do when fake happens to you?
You pretend in return, or you cry away the blue.

You ask questions, knowing the answers will unfold,
The fake ones will keep the fake on and succeed in this world.

Remind yourself that there is another world
where we all have to go,
That's the real world, and that's the real show.

# HEAL

When your soul is in darkness,
You believe there is nothing left to feel,

And your life feels empty in its starkness,
Reach out and I will help you heal.

Many others have journeyed through these dark places as well,
Engulfed in despair, helplessness and a deep hell.

I am here to extend my hand, lessen your pain,
And help you seek the beauty of the cloud that passes as rain.

When your heart seems empty and you have nothing to feel,
Reach out and I will help you heal.

The road we take is hard and rough,
At times, it may take us to crevices that seem tough.

It's a beautiful journey though road blocks we find,
Just think of the beautiful memories and rewind.

When your heart seems empty and has nothing to feel,
Reach out, my friend, and I will help you heal.

# WORDS OF SILENCE

Powerful stories they tell,
These words of silence.

Feverish, painful and unwell,
Are the words of silence.

The depth of a sigh,
The despair in the cry.

The hollowness in the tear,
The sorrowful legacy of fear.

They all have stories to tell,
These words of silence.

The shutting down of the soul,
In letting go of that hole,

Through absence and acceptance,
The strength required immense,

Has its own stories to tell,
Like these words of silence.

# FOUND

Wasn't it not long ago
When the fingers traced the lips?

Wasn't it not long ago
When the lips sought the fingers?

When the ears touched the heart,
Wasn't it not so long ago?

When the soul whispered sweet nothings,
Wasn't that too not long ago?

In seeking, so much was lost
Or was so much found?

# ENDLESS LOVE

It's a warm, dark winter night,
A star shines over, ever so bright.

A moment arrives and holds itself tight,
A thought so strong, it carries in the light.

Loved so many, lost many more,
With laughter, happiness and tears galore.

Some walked away, leaving one ashore;
Some carried through, touching the core.

Endless love, so many around;
Some swam through, some drowned.

Some so dull, some left one spellbound,
Some so boring, some so profound.

Love, that love that is felt by all,
Lasts endlessly, with or without a fall.

It makes you so joyous, yet it makes you crawl,
Can you ever just let it be? Can you stall?

That love we chase, that hole we fill,
Love is within us, we need to keep still.

No emptiness will ever be there to kill,
It's all inside us, and it will fulfil.

Falling in love is beautiful indeed.
Fall in Love within; plant that seed.

Let that love fulfil, let it feed.
Love yourself so deeply, that's all you will ever need.

# UNPEEL

---

Come out, unpeel the seal,
Causing darkness; that's not a deal.

Drop it some day;
How long do you think it will stay?

That pretence, it's yours not;
It's layered with darkness; it's what you got.

Unless this is you, you are that face,
That changes with time and causes disgrace.

It will drop off some day, that mask you wear,
In the dark night, you will unmask, and no one will care.

But drop it, you will; that's the promise of the night,
One person, two faces; some day you will drop that fight.

# FRIENDSHIP

A long time ago, they parted ways,
They knew nothing permanent ever stays.

Betrayals, sadness, insecurities loomed,
Even happiness seemed to struggle, negatives bloomed.

Then one day, they bumped into each other on the street,
They looked at each other and knew they were meant to meet.

Years of denial had taken its toll,
Eyes watched, as the tears decided to roll.

Suddenly, they saw what others couldn't see,
The real friendship, it was always there, hiding willingly.

So, they stared at each other as long as they could,
Felt the layers peeling, all the bad and the good.

When it was all clear with nothing left to feel.
They knew their friendship had lasted, now they would heal.

# WOMAN, RISE

Words like poison spewed,
Perhaps from an internal storm that brewed?

Astonished, she sat there, trying to calm it down,
Totally unexpected was the arrow; down came the crown.

Self-doubt made an appearance and stayed for a while,
Quietly, she bore it all, so not her style.

The viciousness of the attack left her like a rag doll,
But she is a woman; women rise higher after a fall.

Purposefully, stronger than ever, she decided to rise;
She would be who she is; she won't pay any other price.

Threats, projected emotions could stay with them as they pleased;
Anger, hurtful words, mountainous egos would be seized.

Finally letting go of the memories of those words and cries,
Standing tall, as a woman should, she could only rise.

# THE TICK TOCK OF THE CLOCK

3 am and the sound goes tick tock,
Pushing and prodding to take stock.

Chapters need to be laid to rest,
Moving into a world of love—only the best.

Leave behind all the negativity around,
Invite only the energy, and do not be bound.

Hurt will be caused, heart will burn.
Stories will be left, pages will turn.

New stories will be written from the magic within,
Bringing in laugher, love and magical sin.

Authenticity will give rise to an authentic you.
Allow it to be felt as a promise to renew.

# PUNISHMENT

---

"Stop. Please stop. I have young children. I will die", she begged. The beatings didn't stop on that nightmarish night of absolute fear, humiliation and near death.

In the large two-storey home, in a faraway land, the night had turned. Jealousy had shown its dark face and its tentacles had spread. The little girl was now a young woman with children. She was being punished. She had moved on from her marriage a while ago and yet she had still retained her married name. That was the cause of violence that night.

A drunken storm had decided to make its presence felt.

Violence had arrived in the storm, through the storm. The dark night seemed even darker. The large house suddenly too small to keep the little young woman safe.

She ran from one room to the other, hiding, petrified. She could feel her nose bleeding. She ran into the conservatory and hid under the table. She could hear the sound of the computer and the silence of the night and then the footsteps. So close. So close. Suddenly, she felt herself being pulled by the hair and then the hard kicking started – some landing on her private parts in those Doc Martens boots. The little young woman screamed in pain and terror. "Stop, please stop," she cried.

She ran upstairs and hid in the en-suite of her bedroom. Sweat and blood poured out of her in the cold winter night. She could hear the footsteps and her own heartbeat. She wanted her heart to stop beating so she wouldn't be caught. But the heart continued beating and she was caught. The en-suite door was broken down and there was another kick, on her face this time. She cried, she begged. She felt her nose break.

She ran downstairs, screaming all the time. She ran towards the phone to call the cops. The phone was yanked off its hook. She ran to the lounge to get her cell phone. The cell phone was grabbed and thrown outside in the dark.

Finally, she surrendered. There was nothing she could do. She was beaten. She couldn't remember anything beyond this about that night. She was in and out of hell all night.

The morning was different. When she opened her eyes, she saw hell around her. Her beautiful home had been destroyed. She couldn't walk. Her body had been damaged. She couldn't think. Her spirit had been killed. She was alive but she was dead.

She had allowed a storm in. Storms leave destruction. No matter how much it may try not to, that is a storm's role in the universe - to change everything around it and leave a trail of destruction. And that's what the storm had done. Jealousy is perhaps just another word for a storm.

She lived in guilt in the dark recesses of her mind. She had left her marriage, so perhaps she deserved this punishment, she thought.

She was a kind soul but the pain she had put her family through from the choices she made lived in her and she found ways to punish herself.

She deserved this storm she thought, as she passed out, repeatedly that night.

The little young woman remembered the decision to allow storm in her life. Perhaps we allow toxin in our life at a subconscious level, to hurt, to feel pain so we can punish ourselves.

This soul she had allowed into her life, was a stormy one, carrying messages of destruction. This storm caused absolute chaos. Not only did it break up the little young woman's calm life but left very little of her when it was done. The humiliations and embarrassments, the deep pain, suffering, loneliness and scars it left, destroyed her. She was beaten in every way possible. All alone, in a world of her own, away from everyone, she had died.

Many asked why she would do this to herself. She had no answers.

But how many of us have control over storms? We can run away from them, but if we are caught in them, there are only two ways out. Death. Or life.

She chose death. Then life chose her again. It took nearly a decade to find life again.

**The little girl had somehow found her punishment.**

# WORDS OF GRACE

If you find me on the floor,
With everything shut, including the door,

With a broom in my hand and a frown on my face,
I am simply sweeping broken words with grace.

Those words there, what do they say?
"I have moved on in every way."

And those words there, what's in them?
Empty promises, broken dreams, oh don't let them overwhelm.

Ah, I found you hiding in there,
"I don't love you anymore," hiding behind that chair.

And you, "Let's not lose all that we had."
These words? "Is that all we shared?"

Your hurtful words, "I can't take the pain anymore."
Did you think I was dancing and laughing on that floor?

My words, humble, sincere and drunk neat,
I now sweep, put them in that empty box and delete.

If you find me on the floor,
With everything shut, including the door,

With a broom in my hand and a frown on my face,
I am simply sweeping the broken words with grace.

# WARRIOR

Stepping out of her duvet finally,
She put her feet on the floor.

A jolting pain seeped through her body,
As she ran towards the door.

She had stepped on her broken pieces,
Some of them sharp as knives,

Most of them from her past losses,
The ones we carry all our lives.

She walked back to that place again
And stepped on them by choice.

As she let them pierce through her and welcomed the cries,
She let them heal: all those lies.

Eyes closed, she reflected,
On the broken pieces of yesterday.

She had moved on and reconnected,
She knew this warrior was here to stay.

# FOOTPRINTS WITHOUT TOUCHING THE FLOOR

My feet, they didn't touch the floor,
Yet they left footprints at the door.

That door was half open, partly shut;
Tip-toeing, my feet filled up that soulful hut.

Peeping through the doors within that soul,
Something pierced through, as I looked through the hole.

Gently rocking on that chair on the side
Was that soft, sensitive heart, finding a place to hide.

There in the other corner was that little tear,
Working its way to freedom, still withered in fear.

A tiny ounce of light shone through the window.
A little happiness was seeping through; where should that go?

In there, I left a few little pieces of me.
Letting them scatter, I waited until they felt free.

With sadness and joy, these feet left that hut.
Gliding through, the doors they gently shut.

The feet, striding silently floated through that door,
Leaving footprints without touching the floor.

# LIGHT IN THE DARK

Guided in the dark,
Following that spark.

Tunnel is in sight.
Glimpse of light?

Feet hesitate: to walk or not?
Reminding of darkness it's fought.

Nah, stop, it says once more.
Follow only the light within your shore.

The other light only follows the dark.
The light within is always lit; you don't need a spark.

# THE SHUT DOOR

The door was left open,
Allowing laughter, love and fun.

Then storms arrived to kill,
Causing devastation, leaving nothing still.

The locks came out and put firmly now.
No strangers within does it now allow.

The strangers are now met outside this door;
They can bring their storm, and they can roar.

Destruction, devastation, remain outside this line,
Through this, the sun inside continues to shine.

Detachment: that's the name of the game,
Allowing only those who respect the same.

The soul shines. The love continues,
The joy this brings multiplies the hues.

That door that has now been shut
Houses joy and beauty inside that little hut.

# SHE WAS READY

Retreating
Peacefully,
She smiled.
The room lit up.

Angels had arrived,
Waiting to carry her.

She was ready.

They bathed her in love,
Soaping her with rosewater,
Rubbing sandalwood paste on her.

They stopped.
They looked at her.
They were struck.

Embracing her
In her newfound beauty,
They left, singing...

"You were ready for the world.
Now the world is ready for you"

She was ready.

# CHIN UP

---

When times are tough in life,
At times you can't see the light.

You try to find peace and all you see is strife,
You seek the sun but only darkness is in sight.

Close your eyes and look within,
Reach for your madness, pull up your chin.

You are a warrior; let yourself know,
Spread your strength wherever you go.

# LOST

It's was a hot, sultry evening. Janpath was bustling as usual; there was a cacophony of sounds. People, vehicles, sellers and even roadside cows joined in to create that noise that typically ended one up in a duvet, with a tablet to stop the headache.

This evening, the young woman was out shopping with a couple of people she had recently met. They wanted to buy the street side pashminas. The young woman tagged along. Strangely, her feet felt like iron; her soul seemed to have become heavy. She was in a different place that evening, she was there, yet she wasn't.

"Oh, what a beautiful pashmina," she exclaimed, excitedly as she took out her phone and dialled the number that was on auto mode. As usual, whenever there was something that arrested her attention (good or bad), it's this number that her fingers dialled. She heard no ring this time. The phone seemed to have been switched off. She tried again....

She felt panic. Why was the phone switched off at 7 p.m. on a Sunday she wondered? She tried another couple of times; sweating, clearly in distress by now.

And suddenly, she stopped. Realization hit her. She felt her body going stiff and colour leaving her face.

She remembered that only two days ago she had been part of her final journey. She had with immense pain, let her go.

She looked into her handbag as if looking inside would change things. She looked at the phone she was trying to ring a minute or two ago.

There would be no more calls to her mother or from her mother. Her mother was in a new place now. Her magic mama had gone.

She let go of the pashmina. Clutching to her mother's phone, she walked away and said, "Please, just one more time. Can I hear your voice? Just one more time, Ma."

**That day the little young girl learnt about emptiness: how one could be in the most crowded places, yet feel alone.**

# FROZEN FLIGHTS

It's been a long while since that fateful night,
That tormented, painful feeling on that torturous flight.

It's agony for any child, in a distant land, to hear that phone bell,
Knowing that some day, it might carry the news from hell.

Hell it was, when the plane landed in our land;
My soul, my heart, my being needed your hand.

Courage had left me, fingers had lost their feel;
Should I put the phone on? What would life deal?

Then the inevitable seemed to have made up its mind;
The universe had delivered its verdict;
life wasn't going to be kind.

When you went away, this memory froze in its haste,
Mother, with you gone, the flights now have a different taste.

Each time she lands, the frozen bit of you comes up to grind,
I take the blessed phone, and a faint hope, I still try to find.

Then my beating heart reminds me that you have gone away,
That these landing through the clouds may be less grave some day.

# MOTHER, MOTHER, MOTHER

**I am you.**
Emotionally,
Intellectually,
Spiritually,
In my soul,
I am you.

My tears without tears,
My happiness, anger, and fears,

My love, loss and gain,
Friends, some not, the pain.

All come from within this hue,
Simply because I am you.

My life is full of life,
Craziness, gentleness, strife.

My emptiness, fullness, attitude,
Your teachings and silent fortitude,

All come from within this hue,
Simply because I am you.

My soul, you gave birth to,
Laughter, sarcasm, and silence too.

My dear mother, you are me.
Or am I you?

All comes from within this hue,
Simply because I am you.

My mother, you will always dwell,
In memories, heavenly stairwell.

My soul, your soul were further united,
You saw fire. Light was sighted.

All this and more comes from this hue,
Because you are me and I am you.

# I HEAR YOU

Moving to my sides, I reached out for you,
Wanting to feel your warmth for a minute or two.

Shutting my eyes, I hear your naughty giggles aloud,
That sound of your laughter, through rain or through cloud.

Sitting up, with my heart beating wildly through my pores,
I heard you calling out my name through those empty shores.

You were gently reminding me of the lessons you taught us all:
Never to bow down to nonsense and never to fall,

Not to pander to egos that so many others carry,
They're theirs to keep and theirs to marry.

Let no one tell you what is right or wrong for you;
Take every advice, but listen to only a few.

May your stillness within give you courage to make choices right,
And not to accept everything that seems right and in sight.

Use your inner strength to live a life that's true;
Every breath that you take, for others joy may it brew.

Snuggling up to my side and taking it all in,
I smelt the familiar fragrance of my mother, her love, of my soul within.

# TIME

Time is made up of time,
And time is simply
Endless moments,
Beautiful memories,
Soulful living,
Kindness in the heart,
Purity in the soul,
Giving,
Learning,
Unlearning,
Sharing,
Loving, loving, loving...
And finding a purpose.

Knowing,
One day,
It will all be boxed,
packed
into time.

# TIME,
# I SALUTE YOU

No one can teach as much as you do,
Learning amidst the grey, the black and the blue.

Big lessons from the little things thrown at us,
Teach us that life can at times be a hazy fuzz.

Time, oh dear time, my respect for you is anew,
This life, time with you, is only promised to a few.

Time, my wonderful friend, I salute you.

# TEA BAG

That tea bag,
When you put to boil.
That's the strong woman,
Rising in her turmoil.

When strong women rise,
Hopelessness, despair, and fear step aside.

Silent strength enters that space;
You will smell that power; fear has no place.

Gently rising, holding that light,
You will feel her presence, even when out of sight.

That tea bag,
When you put to boil.

That's the strong woman,
Rising in her turmoil.

# HOMECOMING

Walking along a treacherous path,
With no ending and many a start,

Finally sighting light in the dark,
Leaving behind all that is stark,

Arriving home, fully awake, although late,
Let the universe its magic create.

# I AM HOME

Keep walking, they say to me.
Where will you take me? What will I see?

You will walk until you reach that home you want,
Until you reach there, only weaknesses you will flaunt.

You will see what no one wants to see,
Just keep walking, my love; home holds your destiny.

# HOME OF MY TWIN SOULS

Often, huddled against the bosom of my dearest mom,
Drifting away blissfully, that would be my home.

Home went away to another world of her own,
Home suddenly collapsed, and only darkness shone.

Home is where the heart is, was told to me;
Heart abandoned multiple times, so home was lost too, you see.

Then a miracle happened; two little souls came my way,
Each bringing in joy together, and home was here to stay.

Their breath became my home, their laughter the pillars;
Everything in-between and beyond felt like fillers.

Home is now the soul of my two little souls,
Each building a nest, each playing their roles.

Today, I wish to be the bosom that they both can call home;
Today, I wish forever, I can give to them this loving dome.

Home is not what you think home should be;
Home is home when your bosom can hold love endlessly.

# IN A BLINK

---

This breath, in a blink, it goes.
Take time to smell that rose.

Stories we remain, characters of life.
Let's spread joy around; let go of strife.

Chapters will go with us, unshared and untold.
Trust more in the universe; let it unfold.

Leave a legacy that will bring the universe to you,
Become stories that others can share of you.

This breath, in a blink, it goes.
Make time; go smell that rose.

# THIS MOMENT

This moment, as colours splashed my face,
As a mother, around my mother, standing in grace.

This moment, I have bottled in my soul.
This stays forever, in this place, beyond this role.

This moment, love was at its best,
With mothers creating, re-creating, and loving their own nest.

This moment has the purity of the forever kind.
It has stayed beyond my heart, my soul and my mind.

# DROPLETS FROM MY SKY

These cheeks felt small,
As they smiled to catch your fall.

Hard to hold these droplets from my sky,
As they watched your eyes say goodbye.

# CASKED GOODBYES

When you don't say goodbye and they go,
Is it still a goodbye? How does one know?

Do we say farewell to the laughter left behind?
Or say ciao to the words left in the mind?

The unfinished conversations, where do they go?
Do we continue with the words, even if no more?

So many questions the heart has asked,
With lingering moments of watching goodbyes casked.

Is there any way to get that one last goodbye?
To give them a hug, say farewell and not cry?

This journey is a life of welcomes and hellos.
With folded hands, stay humble until it goes.

# LIFE

What is short?
Life.

What is long?
Life.

In-between
The short and the long
Is love,
Is life.

Live
Your love.

# COMING HOME

Home.
Is it a place?
A country?
Family?
Children?
House?
Pets?
Friends?
Things?

I keep coming home.
Each time I leave,
Each time I arrive,
Everything and everyone
Who touches my soul
Feels like home.

For a bohemian like me,
Home is something I carry,
Inside me.

Every brick is built with
Love,
Experience,
Imperfection,
And learning.

My home
Is
Me.

# WALKING HOME

You hold on,
You hold back,

Masking the pain,
Masking the love,
Masking every emotion
That you have.

Then the time arrives
When time has no time left.

Your entire being—
Every cell—
Sits back and accepts.

Just say,
Just be.
Cry if you must,
Laugh if it feels right.
Live now,
Live fully.

Embrace,
Engage.
Feel,
Share.
Live your truth.
Go, love.

We are, after all,
Only just walking
Each other home.

# SEEKING HOME

Looking at the walls that surround,
This gentle, crazy life.
Walls are built, bridges around,
At times, magically useful strife.

Feeling homesick, looking for parts of me,
I swiftly scan the place.
They remain within the full and empty me
As I live this life, amazed.

Is it a person, a place or thing,
That holds me in this chain?
Why is it that my heart doesn't sing?
Why does it feels this strain?

I stop myself, seek within and build that fireplace,
Where love is what we create, in this magical space.

This room, will keep the warmth and push the coldness away,
Create a home within my home where all our love can stay.

# THE MOON REFUSED...

Last night, the moon refused to show her sight;
It felt dark within, without her light.

I asked why would she do that to me,
She responded, "You have your own light. You don't need me."

I sighed. I cried. I fought with all my might,
Until I stopped, felt her within, and found it, to her delight.

Tonight, I saw her again, smiling gleefully at me,
I smiled back, told her, "You wait, and you will see."

One day, you will be a star somewhere up there,
Whilst I will be the moon, and at me you will stare.

I will hold you in my warmth, and I will carry all your shine.
I will be the light of the universe, of the love divine.

# LIFE, I LEARNT

Life will give us life in doses,
Life will be a bed of thorns on roses.

Teaching us things that we need to unlearn,
Making us want what we don't get, making us yearn.

It teaches us that although the intent may not always be bad,
Some will hurt you, cause pain and make you sad.

It teaches us that not everything we know is always true.
That what we see, what we think has another perspective too.

It will teach us to bid farewell without warning and pay a price.
Goodbyes will happen when they're meant to
and catch us by surprise.

Life teaches us that happiness is not the only goal.
Hurt, pain, anger, grief, all will play their role.

Love will come, love will go.
What will stay is what we know.

Friends will last as long as friends do.
Those who stay will really just be a few.

Life teaches us to be wise and kind.
Some we love and we keep, some we say, never mind.

# TRUTH AND LIE

Forever
And
"This moment"

One truth.
One lie.

The lie
Brings a cynical smile.

The truth
Makes one want to fly.

# REMEMBERING

In me, you live.
Yet I miss you
As I miss that part of me
That left with you.

I try to seek you in deeds,
Just as you taught me,
Through actions of kindness
So we can be free.

Yet each passing day,
I crave that which you took with you,
Your silly laughter, mad giggles,
That evening rum and stories of you.

Maybe just today, I will celebrate that part of us
That laughed and talked and smiled at all the fuss.
Maybe for today, I will pretend to be you,
Laugh at this silly world, and keep the magic anew.

# HOME IS IN YOUR ARMS

"Is this home?" I asked the cloud,
Silently, then thinking out loud.

It feels so safe, eyes open and shut,
Calmness seeping from within the gut.

Total surrender, control handed over to someone,
Sitting back, peace within, no desire to run.

"Yes, this must be your true home," said that voice within,
"Up in my arms, no fears," said the cloud with a grin.

# INK

Closing my eyes,
I used the ink
From my soul
To draw a picture
Of love.

I opened my eyes.
It was
**YOU**

# SEEKING

In moments,
I seek life.

Then I find you.

And each moment
Becomes life.

Becomes me.

I become life.

# UP IN THE CLOUDS

Here,
In this moment,
Surrendering fully,
There is peace.

Life is handed over,
Just in this moment
Of no control.
This is peace.

Floating,
No fears,
In the arms of the clouds.
Only peace.

# WOMAN'S DAY

Let no one tell us that today is our day,
We celebrate our womanhood, each moment, every day.

Tell those who wish us, we need no validation;
We need respect not through words, but through action.

Let's tell ourselves that we are what every woman can be,
Not just mothers, sisters, wives,
daughters; we are love and we are free.

Free from our own shackles that we put around our neck,
Only now realising, oh, what the heck.

Let's stand strong and be that beautiful voice,
Staying silent on love, not becoming the noise.

# OUR DANCE

In the chaotic silence of the night,
(Yeah, you heard that right),

Wild, drunk, noises abound.
Yet silence within—not a sound.

I heard her laugh and saw her come up to me,
Hesitantly she asked, "Will you dance with me?"

Smiling at her, I said, "Absolutely."
Into the night, we danced so beautifully.

Then the time came when the music was left no more,
She looked at me sadly. "Love, I now have to go."

Gently, with happiness, I told her silently so,
"The music has stopped, the dance never needs to slow."

"Go my love, but keep the music in that stride.
Hum the songs; there is nothing to hide.

In the chaotic silence of this beautiful night,
You found your music. Now go find your light."

# US

I close my eyes
And think of you.

I hold on to those moments
Which were few.

Perhaps we were given
A package for two.

We used it all up
Quickly and grew.
Here's what I want from you:

Unlimited packages, unlimited moments
Of just being with you.

# MY LIGHT

We talk all night,
I keep you awake with my light.

My light holds you in its embrace,
Whispering to you with grace.

Softly whispering, the brokenness must be healed,
The incompleteness sealed.

Each night, I come back for you
To say, you will blossom again and feel new.

I am the half-lit moon on my night walk
And you, the tree of life, holding on like a rock.

When I feel low and need to hide,
In your arms, I run and I slide.

Together, we share a common goal;
We carry stories of each and every soul.

So my little strong tree,
Blossom again and be free.

Alone. Together. You and me.
Our purpose is to just be.

# MY
# CLOUDY BAY

Here, waiting,
Debating.

Flying through the cloud,
Another afternoon of thinking out loud.

Up there, it's my abode,
My frequently-travelled road.

Looking out, my fears all melt,
These clouds remember how I have felt.

Endlessly I glide on never-ending flights,
Observing, watching all those sights.

Does it matter at all anymore?
These arrivals and departures or where we go?

Does it matter how long we glide?
Do we really have time on our side?

Waiting, debating, I take it in my stride.
Another day at the airport, in my clouds I hide.

# MOON-KISSED

There was a marvel in the sky last night;
The smiles stayed smiling, as they shone their light.

The sun handed over the light to the moon,
And went off to sleep, perhaps to hold another in a spoon.

The moon arrived - full, shiny and bright,
She whispered sweet nothings through the night.

The moon shared the stories of her day.
She said, "Close your eyes; my stories will make you sway."

Her stories, our stories, all became one,
Closing my eyes, dancing in her light, I joined in the fun!

She took me to places that I had left behind,
With a jolt, I opened my eyes as I heard voices unkind,

Those dark noises came hauntingly in this glistening moonlight,
I forced them away, shut my eyes, pushing darkness out of sight.

The moon then took me to a path I seldom knew,
Look at this love, this magic, this music shared with a few.

Indulging her, I let it flow as she held my hand and said, "Let's go."
We wandered into the mysterious world where we grow.

There were thorns we walked through,
Some still causing hurt, others dead, just as I knew.

There were birds still singing along,
Reminders of the magic, the music and those loving songs.

There were those who were undisclosed, to arrive.
Waiting for the next chapter, will they bring joy or strife?

The moon gently touched my lips and, opening my eyes,
I saw her smiling. Accept this life; smile and you will rise.

I held her in my arms for a gentle second or two,
Getting off the bed, I was ready for light, I now knew!

# FREE THE FIRE

Fire, peace, warmth, heat, soul,
Love, my happiness, your happiness, my goal.

Inside the fire, there is a deeper fire,
To find me, find you, and find our desire.

The soul knows what the heart refuses to see;
this deep longing will never set us free.

I close my eyes and live every bit of you and me,
In my thoughts and dreams, we set ourselves free.

The desire burns every cell of me—my being, my bones,
Your every cell cries out as I hear your moans.

In my thoughts and dreams, that's how we set us free,
And in this is the reality of you and me.

# YOU

---

The tattoo on your hips,
The curving of your lips,
Makes me want to do,
A song and dance or two.

That cheeky, dimpled smile,
Haven't seen it in a while,
It makes me dash off to you,
To spend moments few.

The drunkenness in those eyes,
And those half truths, full lies,
Make me want to be,
The one who can set you free.

That sway in the way you walk,
Your endless chatter and that crazy talk,
Makes me want some more,
To lay in your arms, as we grow.

# YOUR EYES

Drowning in them,
I had to die.

Your eyes,
They don't lie.

A world I see,
A truth I dare.

Is it a lie?
Do I care?

Your eyes,
They don't lie.

Let me drown.
Let me die.

# THE GENIE'S WISH

Not knowing what to do,
I found myself looking for you.

Wearing my funkiest haircut,
And a pair of shades, I left the rut.

I looked into light and dark around;
I looked at the spirits and look what I found.

A magical genie had appeared suddenly;
She decided to share her wishes willingly.

"Only one wish for the day shall I grant you,
Go, my girl, wish for that one thing that is due."

I looked within; I asked that part of me,
"What do I need?" and I knew instantly.

Find me parts of the old me which were solid mentally;
Find me the me that laughed at her fall,
The me that never relented, that was never one to crawl.

Find me that girl whose magic could be seen,
Grant me that wish my genie; let me be evergreen.

# DANCING LIGHTS

---

Just that once, I glimpsed you.
After all, that night you had turned super blue.

Smiling, I sent my message through you.
Your dancing lights embraced us equally, we both knew.

# LOCKING THE LOCKS...

Silently she walks,
Locking the locks,

Wind on her face,
Lines etched with grace,

Half withdrawn,
Half in, half gone,

Within, fully still,
Soul fulfilled,

Asking herself, watching on.
Where have the words gone?

The wind carried them away;
Words are no more left to sway.

Perhaps they're perched up on that bark,
Naked, frightening, words so dark.

Perhaps she left them on that shore,
Words following, as she tightly shut that door.

Maybe, it's all still in her, padlocked.
Those words, how they have mocked!

In silence, she lets them all go,
Words of silence say no more.

# COLOURS

Sometimes when you simply want to hide,
Away from the gushing tide,

You find yourself in black and white.
Everything leaves you, including that inner fight.

You keep looking up for that rainbow,
Breathe in. Close your eyes. And there you go.

Colours, colours, now in your sight,
Red, blue, green, yellow, purple and oh, that white!

When you open your eyes and stare,
All you see are colours everywhere.

# MEETING MYSELF

I bumped into me today,
It was sudden; what can I say?

A passing wind, a passing breeze,
Caught me unawares and on my knees.

Pulling me softly and forcefully by my hair,
It asked me to sit still, let go of despair.

Struggling to settle, not knowing what to do,
I looked away from me and looked towards you.

Your gentle strength delivered to me,
That message to keep the faith, to just be.

Reaching for my hand, I softly heard myself say,
Hey, stay this way, it was great to meet you today.

# MYSTERIOUS GLEE

It creeps into a part of me,
That part which won't let it be.

Embracing it, I allow its curiosity with glee;
It's looking for something even I can't see.

Much have I left behind, nothing is here with me,
Isn't this the reason you see my ecstasy?

Look as you must, but be aware of the mystery,
That what you seek in me is now a complete history.

A sense of calm, a stillness is now me;
Creep in somewhere else where there is a need for you to be.

# LOST AND FOUND

Lost words found their way,
Wondering are they here to stay?

Don't know, can't say,
Night's over; time for the day.

Squashed no more, easily out,
Smiling its way through without a shout.

Giggling, as they walk through the happy door,
Words are singing, please let me out more.

# DANCERS

The dancers have arrived.
They teased that darkness.
Until darkness gave in,
Joined in the medley.
Of colours,
And celebrated,
What was,
What is
And what will be.

# MY BEST FRIEND

She was dark in her being,
Yet light in her presence.
A fan, a follower, was she?
Why else would she be stuck to me?

Some days ahead of me,
Showing me the way.
Some nights behind me,
Pushing me, goading me,
Asking me to stay.

My hurt would be hers,
My anger too.
The pain I felt within,
She would hide it too.

When I laughed with joy,
She would double up as well.
When I cried my tears and my eyes would swell,
Silent or otherwise,
She would hold me, embrace me,

And say, "It's ok. You have me."

When friends betrayed my love,
And lovers stabbed my soul,
She walked with me, beside me,
And slowly let me be whole.

When I lost my will to be,
She looked me in the eye,
Held me, slapped me, kicked me,
But got me to see.

Life is what it is: a beautiful meadow.
The only one you have forever is your own shadow.
Yes, this shadow is the only true friend in this journey,
Mine, yours, ours, for eternity.

# AT THE SAME TIME

Alienated and
Accepted
At the same time.

Loved and
Feared
At the same time.

Those who get me,
Those who don't,
At the same time.

When life happens
And it doesn't,
At the same time.

Remember
And forget
At the same time.

# HOME

Eyes met.
Earth didn't shift.

Bells didn't ring.
Nothing happened.

Yet so much did.
My soul found yours.

We walked quietly.
Passionately, at times.

Words were used,
Silence shared.

Joyfully,
Painfully.
Home had arrived.
In my soul,
I am home.

# TWILIGHT

In between the rising
And the setting.

Meet me there.

I am waiting.

In the twilight
Of my being.

# VISITOR

She dropped by
For a while.
In her usual
Confident style.

She caught me
Inside of me.
She wouldn't go,
Wouldn't let be me.

I allowed her in,
Indulged in her.
Within me,
She had caused a stir.

She brought me thoughts
As a gift,
Memories of those permanent
And temporary rifts.

Then she dropped
through these eyes,
Smiling indulgently,
Saying her goodbyes.

# HAPPY FEET

My life partners:
You two.

The only ones who carry
My thought.

To places
Known and
Unknown.

Leaving our prints
Seen and
Unseen.

Always dancing,
Happily and
Unhappily.

Together forever,
Thinking and
Feeling.

You are my
Partners
In crime
For life.

# A BILLION STORIES

The billion stories in her smile,
Walking, running, clocking every mile.

Grey in her hair, lines on her face,
Ageing, loving, growing, and learning with grace.

What once was will never again be;
This caged bird is now free.

The scars will never go out of style;
Emotions will simply stay on for a while.

She still has promises to keep,
And a million miles to go before sleep.

# MAGICAL CLOUD

---

It's raining, and the music is loud,
It's finally here: my magical cloud.

My cloud has the rain and the light;
It washes all the negatives in sight.

My cloud, she plays with the sun and the moon;
When tired, she holds herself in a spoon.

She dances, laughs, curses and cries,
When against the storms, she fights, she tries.

My cloud holds the magic to the world;
Life in the cloud is my love unfurled.

# MY JOKER FACE

The moon was watching;
So was the sun.

It was that beautiful time
In-between,
The moon passing the baton,
The sun ready,
My feet mystically walking.
I saw her,
Beautiful in her shine.
I sat.

My fingers were playing;
It didn't matter that there was no music.
We both felt it;
Then I looked,
And I smiled.
The smile was returned.

It was a mirror.
Look what I found!

A joker was staring back,
Smiling at my journey,
Mocking me playfully.

Share in my glee;
Enjoy this life, my friend;
Treat it like a tree.

Live it fully,
Purposefully.
Laugh, cry and just be.
Stay grounded and strong,
Spread your branches,
Shed the dry leaves
And give shade to the passer-by.
Hold on to the lessons,
Stay wild
And stay a child.

# EGOS THAT CRAWL

Tired, exhausted, crawling through,
Getting rid of old, bringing in the new,

Questioning the very purpose of the fight,
Which feels strange and does not sit right.

Surrounded by egos the size of boulders unfurled,
Who think that they are God, that they are the world.

What does it all mean? Do they even know?
What stays now is here; all else will go.

Unlearning the learning and learning the new,
It is the truth for the evolved; those left are few.

Smiling through it all, when the egos are thrown,
What is their purpose? Why haven't they grown?

When such questions clutter the mind,
Let those poor starving beings be. Just be kind.

For tomorrow may not be what it seems to be today,
It's a matter of time, as night will never be day.

# WHISKY, TEA AND ME

I am not everyone's cup of tea,
Nor anyone's cup of coffee.

I am not anyone's glass of lassi,
And not everyone loves me.

Whether lassi, coffee, or tea,
If you want it dull, then definitely it's not me.

So am I an endless glass of whisky?
Peaty, smoky, and making you feel heady?

Am I that endless glass of wine?
A few glasses of me, and it all tastes divine.

Guess which of me is everyone's me:
Tea, coffee, lassi, wine or that smoky, peaty whisky?

# NOTHING I OWN

When you asked
For my heart,
I told you
At the start:

Nothing is mine.
That's why I shine.

Not this heart.
Nor this body.
Not this joy.
Nor the pain.
Not this love.
Nor this spirit.

Even my words,
I don't own.
With this learning,
I have grown.

All I own is my soul.
And that's my role:
To keep it polished,
Pure and flourished.
After all, it is that
Which will carry me home.

You can keep my heart,
Together or apart.
It wasn't mine to own;
You and I have always known.

# A PROMISE

You were beautiful, amazing and an adventure of my soul,
I leave you behind as I continue towards my goal.

Of finding me, of seeking she who lies inside,
Thank you for being my friend, my guide.

You gave me big highs and even deeper lows;
Feelings of deep pain, anger and emotions arose.

Life seemed beautiful in your presence and empty as you go;
The new year promises new beginnings galore.

This new year is a promise to me, to my soul to be free,
To unlock that cage that imprisons me,

To fly across the sky, climb those mountains and face myself,
This will be an amazing year of adventure, beauty, love and self.

# WILD

---

Let's not test
the gentleness
of the wild.

Their ferocity
will scare
the storm.

# TOGETHER

---

Gently,
I gaze into you.

Softly
I feel your soul.

Fondly,
I hold your hands.

Warmly,
You take it all.

Happily,
We laugh, we share,

Knowing
We are home.

# THROUGH YOUR EYES

Holding you gently, feeling you within,
Life felt beautiful, lived with a grin.

With eyes wide open, the world I can see,
Where you can be you and I can be me.

Holding you closer, I walk with my eyes,
Observing the masked dance, the untold lies.

I watch that gentle man, leaning against the stall;
He looked totally happy, but his life had hit a wall.

His bank was empty, his wife had left,
How many nights in his empty bed he had wept.

Eyes watched him forcing on a smile,
Letting the other masks admire his style.

That lady by the door, surrounded by them all,
Will they be around when her mask will give up and fall?

Do they know how alone she really felt?
Would they still laugh at her sadness? Would they melt?

As we hold and walk up to the floor,
That couple we see, standing by the door,

Look at the glitter they carry around,
Not just the diamonds, but the jewelled masks, surround.

Do they even know, and do they even care?
The truth cannot be hidden by the diamonds that they wear.

Observe the light and the dark, as I walk you in my land,
The truth, the lies, the mask remain, as we walk hand in hand.

# LOVE
# FELL IN LOVE

Today, love fell in love with me,
Finally, it all made sense; I felt ecstasy.

All I had to do was simply shut my eyes
And count all those moments of truth and lies.

Inside me, there she was, holding her light
And smiling away, despite the drops falling out of sight.

Momentarily, time stretched until it swept through me,
The pure reflection of life around, blissfully free.

With it came something else that engulfed me,
A sense of solitude that comes; it's not a fantasy.

Listening carefully, the voice called out clear and loud,
Come, it said, hit me here, bring that rain, that cloud.

No matter what greyness comes to swallow me,
My light, that peace, will be my ecstasy.

# BOTTLE OF LIFE

That which took years
Dropped by suddenly.

No knocks,
No warnings.

Disappeared
Suddenly.

Hushed silence,
Still night,
Maybe a bottle of life.

Nothing,
Suddenly.

It all left
Suddenly.

She smiled
Suddenly.

When she lit,
All was blue
Suddenly.

# HER
# AND I

She stayed with me all night,
Bringing with her, the much needed light.

Loved me, soothed me, played with my hair,
So much loving, so much care.

Then when it was time for her to go,
She held me closer, even more.

Said, she would come back for me another day,
I let her go, I had nothing to say.

# US

In the growing up,
And in growing,
Somehow,
I missed
Knowing.

And the
Us of Us
Never grew.

One day
Suddenly,
You went away.

Just as
I was nearly
Becoming
You
In our way.

Now I am
You

And I seek
Me.

In me
Of the us
I find me.

# IMAGINE

Imagine
For a little while.

We indulge
In a little lie.

We pretend
It's just you and I.

We connect
And get our high.

We let go
Of the why.

We accept
we sigh.

We live
And we die.

# MOMENTARILY

---

Crossed my path
Momentarily.

Caught in the mesh
Momentarily.

Like glue, we stuck
Momentarily.

With total belief
But momentarily.

Like glass, we broke
Permanently.

Moments shattered
Permanently.

# MY TWO NOSE PINS

These two: one stud, one ring,
So much of me to life, they bring.

The stud gives me the stamp of life,
The ring helps me like the double-edged knife.

Now you must think: what can a nose pin do?
Think about it, one with two pins, only a few?

What does it say when you have two instead of one?
Maybe it has no meaning, perhaps it's just fun.

Perhaps it's a discovery of a journey that has been,
One person, two worlds, one seen, one half-unseen.

These nose pins carry a tale of two;
One says what it does, the other lets it brew.

The one with the stamp, it leaves its mark,
The one with the ring brings light when dark.

That's the story of my two nose pins,
They are the collection of my multiple sins.

# WORDS

Words
Need a free day.

To not do,
Not say.

To just be
In whatever way.

Laugh, cry
Or have a holiday.

Words
today.
Let's just
Lay.

Let's hug
Each other in a way.

That makes
Us both stay.

# Q&A OF LIFE

In the why and the how,
We forget the now.

In the when and the what,
How much have we fought?

In the who and the where,
Do we even care?

Question: Why do we?
Answers, let them be.

Sitting back, walking past,
Realisation hits. Nothing lasts.

No more questions, no answers still,
Let it be. Let it not kill.

No why, what, when, where or how.
Live fully. To life, let's bow!

# 3 AM'S LOVE FOR 2 AM

3am arrived at 2am's door,
It was just like in nineteen ninety four.

They chatted about the moon for a bit,
Then 2 am asked 3am to relax, to sit.

3am asked if 2am remembered that particular date,
When life took a turn, and wrote it's fate.

2am, looked deeply in 3am's eyes,
Said it can't lie, that love it can't disguise.

Their pact to be chiquita's of the soul,
She had lived it, and made it her goal.

Coffee was called, to deliver it's news,
Cookies sauntered in to share it's views.

All four, sat in silence and in sound,
Thinking of all the losses, and what they had found.

3 am and 2 am quickly shared a smile,
Knew meeting like this, it was all worthwhile.

3 am got a call from 4 am, asked her to come around,
2 am quietly said, "not today please" without a sound.

Holding hands, these two sat chatting through the night,
Finally, when 8am appeared, they disappeared out of sight.

If you find two chiquita's, holding on to nineteen ninety four,
Take them home, shower love, and gently shut that door.

# LOVE OVERDUE

Love knocked on my door,
It was, I think, ten past four.

It caught me gently by my hair,
Awestruck, I simply continued to stare.

It hit me in my gut so hard,
Intuitively I knew, magic was on the card.

I tried to run away from this force anew,
Love smiled and said, "I think I am overdue".

# MAGIC

I hid myself behind the flour tin,
Love looked at me, pulled me out with a grin.

"Stop, you girl, let me stay,
In this magical gentleness let us sway.

Hold your faith in me and the message I bring,
Let me be your lover, and not a fling".

Slowly, I let myself out of my hidden spot,
I looked at love, and said, "show me what you got".

Love, held my hand showed me it's loving side,
Said, "can we weave magic, let love win, please don't hide".

# THE STORY THAT STARTED THE LIES...

The little girl now a mature young woman, driving through a Wellington road in her small, comfortable four-wheel drive was exceptionally sad this morning. The rough night did not bother her. The fact that she was putting her family through so much pain was killing her. The image of her mother standing with that shiny blade in her hand last night played in her mind over and over again.

She had lived an honest life, she knew. She had been rebellious perhaps by some people's definition, but she had lived an overall well-balanced, dutiful life. She had lived as she was expected to, by the rules.

She had married by choice and had done all that one would within the marriage.

Yet, she knew, this wasn't her truth. Her life perhaps was always going to be a lie. As she drove, she wondered, would she ever have the courage to speak her truth?

Her thoughts went back to that night when at the insistence of a friend, her usual anti-social self agreed to go out dancing. She joined her friends at an upmarket pub, straight after work that

Friday night. Friday was dress down day, which meant jeans, a black tee and a maroon jacket that she loved. She hardly wore any jewellery other than lots of silver rings on her fingers. Make-up was minimal, with kohl in the eyes and her usual favourite shade of lilac on her lips. There was nothing exceptional about her, except that, as a rule she always upped her energy levels when she stepped out.

That night was no different - mad banter, drinking, music and so much fun with the girls. Her friends were just as fun. Their night outs were always refreshing and it felt wonderful for the young woman to hang out with them, every now and again.

The pub was trendy, with the usual Friday night crowd. People hanging out with their work mates, friends, young party hoppers and the older ones, watching observing and just having their usual night out.

It was just another usual Friday night. Or was it?

And suddenly, in that moment, life seemed to have stopped. She felt herself being drawn to a force beyond her. There in that room, her brown eyes met blue ones. That soul theory that she talked about had arrived. The biggest part of her soul had made its presence felt. It was electrifying. There in that moment, no bells rang. But the music, the noise and the banter seemed to fade away. All she sensed was this being, this presence, this magnet, this magic.

Slowly, she felt herself getting off her seat and moving towards that person. Their eyes had already met. Now their hands shook, smiles were exchanged and the music started again.

"You Fill up My Senses" was playing. She wasn't even asked to dance. They both just naturally moved to the floor together and swayed to that song. No words were exchanged. She could feel her dance partner's breath on her and she wanted to feel more. She felt herself being drawn so deeply by a force she had never experienced before. Her soul was rejoicing and at the same time danger bells were beginning to ring. After all she was not available anymore. She stopped and moved away abruptly. She was followed and no words were spoken yet.

This continued through the night and finally it was time to go home. Her friends had started teasing her and wondering what was going on. She had started feeling good and bad at the same time. She went home without sharing any words or exchanging any numbers. She was relieved that now there would be closure to that feeling and no more worrying about what was right or wrong.

That night when she left for home, she let her mind wonder about the soul theory she believed in but only for a few seconds. Real life was awaiting her at her home.

That moment, however, had stayed with her and she had bottled it into a little soul box and left it there so that she could bring it out during her dark days. As the days went by, she had sealed that box and she had decided she wasn't going to think about it.

She was so wrong in believing that things were always in our control. The universe has its own way of making souls meet when it's time. She had a soul theory that she had believed in all her life. She believed that just like the big bang theory, our souls also went through a big bang experience just before they chose a body to enter. One soul got fragmented into multiple pieces and spread itself into multiple bodies across wherever they were meant to be, in various sizes. Some souls received a minuscule part of that soul piece and some received larger parts. She truly believed that all through our lives our soul seek to unite with those other parts of itself. That is why we acknowledge random strangers, we form friendships and we fall in love.

This soul can have both parts - a light part and a dark part. Perhaps the dark part of our soul connects with some dark part of another soul and that's when we experience conflict with some people, no matter how hard we try not to. But the biggest belief she had was about the biggest part of our soul. She believed, with total intensity that we spend our life looking for the biggest piece of our soul, at a subconscious level. When that coming together happens, the souls know; the universe announces it to the soul in its own way.

She recollected how a few days later a message arrived from that dancing partner. Somehow her number was sought and here they were, now exchanging words. Those words had intensity and depth; like they were waiting for her all her life, waiting to be written for someone. Those were the words the mother and husband had found. They had grown to share more and more of each other, with each other and over time expressed their attraction for each other. She was still caught in the right and the wrong of it all and on a daily basis she tried so hard to run away from this, this feeling and the sensations that it was causing, the turmoil it was creating in her. She avoided it and yet it was there: fully present, fully aware.

As she drove that sad morning, she knew she had to make

a decision.

She couldn't prolong this choice any more. She had known it for many years now. There was no turning back. It was inevitable. The universe had connected her with the biggest part of her soul and she had been forced to feel and to accept.

**She had fallen in love.**

With a woman.

Would she ever speak the truth or would she live her untold lies?

**That day, that young woman knew that she would now be judged for the rest of her life.**

# SHACKLED

**Chained within,**
The shackles powerfully thin.

**Heavy weight,**
Burdened, feel like an inmate.

**Soul cries,**
Live your truth, why these lies.

**Social norms?**
How to break these storms?

**Turmoil inside,**
Can't this be an easier ride?

**Love after all,**
Who is this society that it makes us crawl?

**Life in shackles,**
Is how I will live, my heart crackles.

**Universe unfold,**
Will my truth win, will love hold?

# ACKNOWLEDGEMENTS

There are many people who have shaped my life. The biggest influence and magic has come from my dear Mother who I carry in me, each moment. I have struggled to live without her and now I make an extra effort to live by her principles. I hope to make my mother proud of me, always. This book and all my words are dedicated to her.

To my father, of whom I only have vague memories and who remains in the soul of the little girl who spent all her waking hours weaving stories, lying next to her Dad. Over the years I have understood that people behave in a certain manner based on their circumstances. I have no idea what those were for my Da, or how they affected his behaviour. I have made my peace with it and all I know is that I love you Da.

To my twins Aana and Aash (I call them Ragalets. They are the dualities that represent me fully), who brought magic into my life the day they chose me to be their mother. Their acceptance of me and their encouragement to share my journey have been instrumental in bringing life to this book. I have learnt unconditional loving, thanks to them both.

To my partner Nicola, who allows me to be who I am. She has reviewed all my words a thousand times and she patiently listens each time. Thank you for being my rock and for your unwavering wisdom, love and support.

To the father of my children Ravi, whose unconditional love has always given me wings to fly. Thank you. I am always here for you. We never really left each other; our relationship just evolved into something deeper and meaningful.

To my siblings Oscar and Ophelia, who remain in my soul no matter where I go.

Thank you also to my dear friend Shreya Jha for her support and help with the most important aspects of the book.

A big thank you to all my friends and family who encourage me to live my life unconventionally and who have helped me with the tips for this book, the networks and simply by being in my life and letting me be me.

To the publisher, Embassy Books and its fantastic team. Sohin Lakhani – you are the best, thank you. Aruna, Safa and Ruhi, so much gratitude and appreciation, thank you.

I cannot forget Biscuit, our Bombay cat, who now lives in London. He sat with me for hours during the entire book journey. He is always with me. Thank you Biscuit.